Blue Sky
STUDIOS

THE PEANUTS MOVIE

Movie Novelization

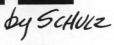

Based on the *Peanuts* comic strip created by Charles M. Schulz
Adapted by Tracey West

Simon Spotlight
New York London Toronto Sydney New Delhi

SIMON SPOTLIGHT
An imprint of Simon & Schuster Children's Publishing Division
1230 Avenue of the Americas, New York, New York 10020
First Simon Spotlight hardcover edition September 2015
© 2015 Peanuts Worldwide LLC © 2015 Twentieth Century Fox Film
Corporation. All rights reserved.
All rights reserved, including the right of reproduction in whole or in part
in any form. SIMON SPOTLIGHT and colophon are registered trademarks
of Simon & Schuster, Inc. For information about special discounts for
bulk purchases, please contact Simon & Schuster Special Sales at
1-866-506-1949 or business@simonandschuster.com.
Designed by Nicholas Sciacca
Manufactured in the United States of America 0815 FFG
10 9 8 7 6 5 4 3 2 1
ISBN 978-1-4814-6044-6 (hc)
ISBN 978-1-4814-4136-0 (pbk)
ISBN 978-1-4814-4137-7 (eBook)

CHAPTER ONE
SNOW DAY!

The first snowflakes fell right at dawn. They tumbled down from the gray sky, along with one fluffy yellow bird.

Woodstock somersaulted through the air, trying to dodge the snowflakes. But they settled on his wings, slowing him down. He came in for a landing on top of a pile of snow. A large, dog-shaped pile of snow.

The mound of snow underneath the little bird exploded, sending Woodstock shooting up into the air. When he landed again, he was on top of a doghouse—and face-to-face with a black-and-white beagle.

Snoopy let out a happy cry and the two best friends hugged. It was going to be a good day.

Snoopy and Woodstock were the first to wake up in the neighborhood, but the others weren't far behind. Alarms rang from house to house as kids got up to get ready for a day of school.

Marcie groggily sat up, put on her glasses, and turned off the alarm.

Over at her house, Peppermint Patty sprang up and grabbed the hockey stick by her bedside. Then the freckle-faced girl used it to smash her alarm clock to pieces.

At Schroeder's house, the blond-haired boy slowly woke up to the calming sounds of classical music written by his favorite composer. He sat up and smiled.

"Ahh. Beethoven."

And in a house nearby, Lucy Van Pelt was up and out of bed like a shot, as always. She went straight into her brother Linus's room. He was still sleeping peacefully, clutching his pale-blue blanket in his arms.

"Linus, time to get up," she whispered.

Linus kept sleeping.

"You don't want to be late for school," Lucy warned gently.

But Linus still didn't wake up. Lucy's dark eyes narrowed. She yanked the blanket away from him.

"GET UP!" Lucy yelled.

Linus leaped out of bed. "Ah! My blanket!"

Next door, at Charlie Brown's house, the phone rang. His little sister, Sally, answered it.

"Hello?" she asked.

"*Waa waa waaa,*" said the voice on the other end.

"Snow day?" Sally repeated. Could it be true? It was! "Snow day!"

Sally let go of the phone and jumped into the air.

"No school today!" she cheered. Then she picked up her schoolbooks from the kitchen table and happily tossed them into the garbage can.

Word of the snow day spread like wildfire around the neighborhood. Minutes later, kids began to stream out of their houses, dressed in winter coats, mittens, and scarves. They carried hockey sticks and ice skates. Snoopy and Woodstock watched as they ran past the doghouse, headed for Charlie Brown's house. Snoopy broke into a happy dance. Snow days were so much fun!

The kids began to talk excitedly.

"Franklin and Peppermint Patty are on my team!" announced Lucy. Whenever they played hockey, Lucy always got to be a captain—and she always made sure she got first pick of her teammates.

"I got my hockey stick!" Schroeder cried, waving it in the air.

"I got my skates!" said Franklin.

"Who has the pucks?" Peppermint Patty asked.

Next to her stood a girl named Patty—just Patty. Even though they had almost the same name, it was easy to tell them apart. Peppermint Patty had brown hair and freckles, and Patty had light brown hair and no freckles.

Patty pointed to a boy walking toward the group. Even though it was snowing, clouds of dirt puffed up as he walked.

"Here comes our goalie!" she called out as Pigpen approached.

Patty's best friend, Violet, shook her head. "Pigpen, were you born dirty?"

Pigpen ignored the comment. He looked at Charlie Brown's house. "What's taking him so long?"

"Come on, Charlie Brown!" the others yelled.

Inside the house, Charlie Brown struggled to put

on his winter gear. In the spring, summer, and fall, getting dressed was so much easier. He just slipped on black shorts and his favorite yellow shirt with the black zigzag pattern, and he was done. But winter was harder. Winter meant boots that he couldn't squeeze over his feet and puffy jackets with a zipper that always got stuck and mittens that he always lost.

The sound of his friends outside faded as Charlie Brown hurried to put on his boots, coat, and hat. When he finally finished, he rushed outside.

"Hey, guys, wait for me!" he cried.

But everyone was gone. They had all left for the pond without him. Charlie Brown's excitement deflated like a balloon.

Then Charlie Brown looked up at the sky. The snow was starting to slow down, and the sun was starting to shine through the parting clouds.

"This could be the day," he said hopefully.

He dashed back inside and grabbed his newest kite. Then he ran down to the open field, which was perfect for kite flying. He jammed the kite into a snowbank and then walked away from it, unraveling the string as he went.

"A new kite, a gentle breeze—it all feels just right," Charlie Brown said. "Now that the Kite-Eating Tree is sleeping for the winter, we have nothing to fear."

Charlie Brown loved to fly kites. But the Kite-Eating Tree always spoiled his fun. In spring, summer, and fall, the tree came alive. Charlie Brown was almost certain that it used its branches like claws to snatch his kites out of the sky. But now that it was winter and the tree was quietly resting, he might just have a chance.

Charlie Brown looked up at the sky again as he unraveled the string. The sun was even brighter now.

"Some days you can just feel when everything is going to turn out all right," he said.

Holding the reel at the end of the string, he faced the kite, which was still sticking out of the snowbank. Then he took a deep breath, turned, and ran as fast as he could.

"Liftoff!" he yelled.

The kite shot out of the snowbank. Charlie Brown looked behind him to see the kite dragging in the snow.

"Wait a minute . . . ," he said, fumbling with the reel. He wrapped some string around it and the kite slowly lifted into the air. Then . . . *whoosh!* A gust of wind picked it up and sent it soaring.

"It's in the air," he said, barely believing it. "It's flying!"

Holding the string, Charlie Brown raced to the top of a nearby hill. The kite soared above him on the breeze. Down below, he could see his friends playing hockey on the iced-over pond.

"Hey, guys! Look! Look! I did it!" he called down. But his friends were too busy with their hockey game to notice.

It didn't matter. The smile on his face grew bigger and bigger. He was doing it!

Suddenly, he felt something yank on his feet. He looked down to see that the string had wrapped around his boots! He lost his balance and slipped, sliding down the hill. He landed on the frozen pond and slid across the ice on his belly like a seal. He finally came to a stop in front of his best friend, Linus.

Linus, still clutching his blanket, looked down at his friend.

"Hey, Charlie Brown. You still can't get that kite to fly, huh?" he asked.

At that very moment a strong gust of wind blew. The kite smacked into the back of poor Charlie Brown's head and then launched into the air, taking Charlie Brown along with it. Linus watched him go.

"Remember, it's the courage to continue that counts!" he called after his friend.

The kite dragged Charlie Brown across the ice at superspeed. The hockey players had to quickly skate out of the way to avoid being hit by him. Charlie Brown managed to get to his feet, holding on tightly to the string. He tried to steer the kite toward the shore.

Up ahead, Lucy was doing figure-skating tricks on the ice, surrounded by a group of kids. She twirled around and then raced across the pond, building up speed.

"And now, for my famous Triple Axel!" she cried. "Prepare to be amazed."

She hopped on her right foot, ready to leap. Then . . . *wham!* Charlie Brown crashed right into her! She twirled three times and landed on her butt as the kids clapped and cheered.

Charlie Brown kept going. He slid across the pond, headed right for a very big tree.

The kite got stuck in the tree, with Charlie Brown still tangled in the string. The string whipped around and around the tree with Charlie Brown still dangling from the end.

Whomp! An avalanche of snow fell from the branches above, revealing old pieces of kites wedged into the branches. When Charlie Brown finally stopped swinging around the tree, he was hanging upside down from one of the branches, next to his kite.

"Ugh," Charlie Brown moaned. "Stupid Kite-Eating Tree!"

Lucy skated up to him, followed by the other kids. "You blockhead!" she yelled. "I should have known. What kind of a person tries to fly a kite in the middle of winter? You will never get that kite to fly. Why? Because you're Charlie Brown!"

CHAPTER TWO
BATTER UP!

Lucy tapped Charlie Brown's forehead. He swung back and forth as he dangled from the tree branch. Then she skated away, and the other kids followed her.

Only Linus stayed behind. He moved to Charlie Brown and placed his hand on Charlie Brown's forehead, stopping him.

"Thanks, Linus," Charlie Brown said.

"Listen, Charlie Brown. Ignoring what my sister Lucy says has enabled me to make it this far in life," Linus said.

Charlie Brown managed a smile. "You're the best,

Linus. What would I do without a good friend like you?"

At that moment Snoopy skated up to Linus. He grabbed Linus's blanket and pulled him back onto the pond, whipping him around by the blanket.

"*Whooooaaa!*" Linus cried.

His hand accidentally grabbed Sally's. Her eyes lit up. Linus, her crush, was holding her hand!

"Aww, my Sweet Babboo!" Sally said, calling him by the nickname she loved to use.

Linus looked back to see that he was holding Sally's hand. He shrieked and dropped it, sending Sally spinning off into a snowbank. Sally sat up and brushed off the snow.

"Isn't he the cutest thing?" she asked with a sigh.

Marcie wobbled as she slowly skated around the pond. Peppermint Patty glided around her, holding a hockey stick.

"Uh, careful, sir," Marcie said, looking past her freckle-faced friend.

Snoopy and Linus whizzed by, and Linus grabbed Peppermint Patty's hand. Then Peppermint Patty's hockey stick snagged Marcie. A game of crack the whip was forming—a line of skaters holding hands as they sped across the ice. One by one, new skaters were pulled onto the line: Frieda, with the naturally curly hair; dark-haired Shermy; Schroeder; Lucy; Franklin; and finally, Pigpen, followed by a cloud of dust.

Zoom! The crack-the-whip line sped across the pond. Woodstock, driving a Zamboni to clean the ice, waved to them.

The kids were going so fast they couldn't hold on to each other anymore. The whip cracked, sending the kids scattering across the ice.

By this time Charlie Brown had freed himself from the Kite-Eating Tree. Still tangled in kite string, he carefully walked across the slippery pond in his boots as his friends skated happily around him.

Charlie Brown left the pond and walked through the snow to the baseball field. He sat down on a bench and began to untangle the string around his body, winding it into a ball as he worked. When he finished, it was the exact size of a baseball.

Inspired, Charlie Brown stood up.

"I don't care what Lucy says. I may have had trouble in the past flying a kite, and I may have never won a baseball game, but it's not for the lack of trying," he said out loud.

He walked around the baseball field, stopping at the snow-covered pitcher's mound.

"My pitching *has* to improve if I come out here to my trusty mound under the snow every day," he said, standing on the mound.

Then he walked straight ahead until he found home plate. He dusted the snow from the plate and then began to build a snowman. It looked like a batter, with a cap on his head and a bat in his hands.

"Charlie Brown is not a quitter," he said, admiring his work. As he marched back to the mound, he looked around. Things weren't quite complete. . . .

Charlie Brown got to work on more snowmen. By the time he finished, he had made eight more baseball players and three base runners and placed them on the field in their proper positions.

Snoopy and Woodstock watched him curiously. Woodstock climbed up and sat in the bleachers, surrounded by mini snowmen. Snoopy donned a baseball cap. Every good team needed a manager.

Snoopy walked out of the dugout, made a snowball, and handed it to Charlie Brown, who nodded and walked back to the pitcher's mound.

"Bottom of the ninth. Two outs. Bases loaded," Charlie Brown said, eyeing the snowman batter. In his mind, he could hear the crowd roar with excitement.

"It all comes down to one pitch," Charlie Brown said. He looked at Snoopy in the dugout, and Snoopy held up one finger.

Charlie Brown knew the signal: fastball. He started to wind up, when Snoopy held up a second finger.

Okay, curveball, Charlie Brown thought. He wound up again. . . .

Then Snoopy held up four fingers and wiggled them.

What's that one, again? Charlie Brown wondered. But before he could even think about another pitch, Snoopy made a peace sign. Then he crossed his fingers. Then he held up all of his fingers and wiggled them.

Charlie Brown shook his head. Snoopy wasn't making any sense, and besides, he didn't need Snoopy to tell him how to pitch.

He had this.

He held the ball behind his back, staring down the batter.

"Let's see if you can handle my fastball," he said.

He wound up. He sent the snowball flying . . . and it rocketed back to him! The snowball batter had hit a line drive without even moving!

Pow! The snowball knocked over Charlie Brown, ripping his clothes from his body.

Pow! The snowball hit the snowman center fielder, and the snowman exploded in a cloud of snow. Then it put a hole in the outfield fence!

Charlie Brown slowly sat up. The tiny snowmen in the bleachers were all frowning. Frustrated, Snoopy threw his hat on the ground.

Charlie Brown lay back down on the snowy mound, staring into the wintry sky.

"It's going to be a long winter," he said with a sigh.

CHAPTER THREE
A NEW NEIGHBOR

The blare of a truck horn got Charlie Brown's attention. He sat up and saw a moving truck rumble down the street. It pulled into the driveway of a house near the baseball field.

"Someone's moving in across the street from me?" Charlie Brown wondered.

Curious to see the new neighbors, the kids ran past Charlie Brown, their ice skates slung over their shoulders.

"Hey, gang, look. There's a new kid moving in!" Franklin called out.

"I'm going to get there first!" someone else shouted as the kids scrambled to be the first to see the new neighbors.

Charlie Brown got up, got dressed, and followed them. They stopped at the wooden fence behind the house and peered through the cracks. Charlie Brown tried to get a view, but he couldn't push his way in.

"Hey, guys. What do you see? Who is it?" Charlie Brown asked.

"Oh! Oh! I think I see a piano!" Schroeder said excitedly. "I hope he loves Beethoven!"

"Beethoven Schmeetoven," Lucy said. She had her own idea of whom the new kid might be—a boy presenting her with a bouquet of flowers and a heart-shaped box of chocolates. "Maybe he will appreciate all my natural beauty."

"Who cares about that?" Peppermint Patty asked. "As long as he's a better goalie than Marcie."

"A goalie, sir?" asked Marcie. "I hope he has a passion for the arts. Shakespeare, da Vinci, van Gogh!"

"That van isn't going anywhere," Sally observed. Then she brightened. "He may have a swimming pool in there!"

Charlie Brown was dying to get a look over that fence. He rolled up a giant snowball and then stood on top of it so he could see. A new kid could mean a new friend! Then he started to worry.

"I just hope this new kid has never heard of me," he said to himself. "He would know nothing of my past imperfections. It's not often you get the opportunity to start over with a clean slate. This time things will be different."

The fence creaked as he leaned over to get a good look. Then . . .

Crash! The wooden fence fell over! The new neighbors could see them!

"*He* did it!" the other kids said, pointing to Charlie Brown. Then they ran off, leaving Charlie Brown standing there all alone to take the blame.

Charlie Brown stood frozen for a moment. Then he ran back to his house as fast as he could.

That night, he talked to Snoopy as he got ready for bed.

"Snoopy, why is it that everything I try turns out wrong?" he wondered. "Sometimes I worry that nobody really likes me."

Charlie Brown crawled under the covers.

"Maybe that new kid will see me for who I really am, like you," Charlie Brown told Snoopy. "A dog doesn't try to give advice, or judge you; they just love you for who you are. It's nice to have someone who will just sit and listen to you."

Charlie Brown turned his head to look at Snoopy— who was snoring away. Then Snoopy rolled over, stealing all the covers from Charlie Brown.

"Man's best friend," Charlie Brown said with a sigh.

CHAPTER FOUR
THE LITTLE RED-HAIRED GIRL

By the next day the sidewalks and streets were clear
of snow, and Charlie Brown and all his friends went to
school. Snoopy walked to school with Charlie Brown.
When they got there, Charlie Brown stopped, knelt
down, and patted Snoopy's head.

"You can't come to school, Snoopy," he said.
"Now, be a good dog and go home."

As Charlie Brown walked up the school steps,
Snoopy quickly put on a disguise—glasses and a big
bow tie. Then he swiped a book from the backpack of
a kid passing by.

Snoopy casually walked up the school steps, hoping to blend in. But Franklin stopped him.

"No dogs allowed!" he said firmly, and closed the door in Snoopy's face.

Snoopy pressed his nose against the glass of the door, dejected. Franklin shook his head.

"What could a dog possibly learn in school?" he wondered out loud. "All they know how to do is eat and sleep."

Snoopy backed away, grumbling. How insulting!

Inside Miss Othmar's classroom, the students were talking in groups before the bell rang. (Everyone except for Peppermint Patty, who was fast asleep at her desk.)

"Did you see the moving van arrive?" somebody was saying.

"Who do you suppose it will be?" asked another.

The classroom door began to open. Everyone got quiet.

"The new kid is coming!" Franklin cried.

But it was only Charlie Brown. A wave of disappointed groans swept through the room.

"Hey, Charlie Brown," Lucy greeted him.

Charlie Brown made his way through the kids and headed to his seat in the back of the room. He passed Linus, who was sitting at his desk with a detailed diorama in front of him. Charlie Brown stopped to get a closer look.

It was amazing! Tiny figures dressed in World War I uniforms moved around an airplane hangar. Sitting on the runway, ready to take off, was a bright red triplane.

"Good morning, Linus. What do you have there?" Charlie Brown asked.

"It's my turn for show and tell today," Linus explained. "This is a model of the same plane flown by Manfred von Richthofen."

"Who?" Charlie Brown asked.

"The Red Baron," Linus replied. "The most famous aviator during the Great War."

"It's not real, is it?" Charlie Brown asked, reaching down. He spun the prop on the plane.

The propeller began to spin. It ignited the tiny gas engine inside the model plane. Then it flew off Linus's desk!

The red plane flew around the classroom, sending the other kids into a panic. Some of them dropped to the floor. Some kids screamed. Papers scattered everywhere.

The plane flew right through Frieda's hair, pulling it straight. "Ah! My naturally curly hair!" she wailed.

The plane flew into a shelf of multicolored jars of paint. They splattered all over Lucy's dress, making her look like a colorful painting. Then it circled back toward Linus's desk.

"Duck, Linus, duck!" Charlie Brown yelled.

The boys dove to the floor and the plane flew right over their heads. Thinking quickly, Marcie opened a window, and the plane flew right out.

"So much for show and tell," Charlie Brown said sadly, and Linus just bumped his head against the window in frustration.

Then the door creaked open again, and the teacher, Miss Othmar, stepped inside.

"Waaa waa wa," she said, unhappy about the kids scattered about the room in strange positions.

"Yes, Miss Othmar," the students said, and then everyone rushed to his or her seat. Marcie got stuck in a cloud of Pigpen dust. She finally reached her desk, coughing.

In front of her, Peppermint Patty was still fast asleep.

"Sir," Marcie whispered, pushing her friend's head forward. But Peppermint Patty's head fell back against the chair.

"Sir," Marcie said louder, pushing her friend's head forward again. This time her head slammed down onto her desk. But that still didn't wake up Peppermint Patty.

"Sir!" Marcie yelled, and Peppermint Patty snapped awake.

"The answer is two! No, three!" She turned to Marcie. "Was I close?"

"Class hasn't started yet, sir," Marcie informed her.

"Waa wa wa waa wa," Miss Othmar announced, and Marcie and Peppermint Patty turned their heads toward the door.

"Waa waaaa wa waa waa," the teacher explained.

"What? The new kid is joining our class?" Franklin blurted out.

A figure appeared in the doorway, lit from behind by the hallway lights. She had long, beautiful red hair and a shy, friendly smile.

"Wow, she's pretty," said Schroeder.

Lucy frowned jealously. "She's not *that* pretty."

Charlie Brown could not take his eyes off the Little Red-Haired Girl. He felt his heart pounding in his chest. He leaned forward to Linus.

"Whoa, Linus," he whispered.

Then he suddenly lifted up his desktop and buried his head inside it, panicked.

"She looked at me," he whispered.

Now he was starting to sweat. But he had to get another look at her. He stared at her through the crack in the desk. Miss Othmar gave her a seat in the front of the room, and he had a perfect view of the back of her head and her long red hair.

Then Miss Othmar interrupted his daydreaming. *"Waa waaa wa waa waaa."*

Everyone moaned and groaned.

"Not the yearly standardized tests again!" someone complained.

Linus stood on his desk and addressed the teacher. Schroeder accompanied him with music on his toy piano.

"Ma'am, will this test accurately reflect the

knowledge we have gained here?" he asked. "Is the test not more of a comment on *your* ability to teach than it is about *our* ability to learn? Is it fair that we at this young age—"

"Waa wa wa waaa!" Miss Othmar interrupted angrily.

Linus sheepishly took his seat. "Yes, ma'am."

He sat back down as the teacher passed out the tests.

Charlie Brown tried to focus on the test.

"'Question one,'" he read out loud. "'If you had six red tomatoes and—'"

Then he stopped and gazed at the Little Red-Haired Girl.

"Red," he whispered dreamily.

Concentrating on the test was going to be impossible!

CHAPTER FIVE
SOMETHING IN COMMON

Charlie Brown stared down at his test paper.

"Come on, focus," he told himself. "First impressions are everything!"

The class worked on their papers, not noticing the intruder approaching them. Snoopy crawled through the air vents until he reached Charlie Brown's classroom. He opened the vent and peeked out. Everyone's heads were down. He was clear.

Snoopy produced a yo-yo and used it to rappel down the wall. Then he slid into an empty seat. He pulled out a binder and began to fill it with papers.

Snoopy smiled to himself. He was sure he looked like a student!

Then he snapped the metal binder rings shut, pinching his finger.

"*Aaaaoooooooo!*" Snoopy howled, and every head in the room turned toward him. He was found out!

Lucy picked him up and marched him to the school's front door.

"No dogs!" she cried, tossing him outside.

Snoopy landed in a trash can filled with old school supplies. As he climbed up out of the pile of junk, something caught his eye.

It was a typewriter. An old-fashioned, clackety-clack typewriter with manual keys. He grinned. Now he could prove to everyone that he wasn't just some silly dog!

Back inside the classroom, Charlie Brown was still filling out his test. He noticed that the Little Red-Haired Girl got up and handed her test to Miss Othmar.

Already done, Charlie Brown thought. *She must be smart.*

As she sat back down, her pencil fell off her desk. It rolled all the way to the back of the classroom and stopped right at Charlie Brown's feet.

Charlie Brown picked it up and admired it. It was a pretty special pencil, pink with a white feather sticking out of the top. Then he noticed something else—teeth marks.

"She nibbles on her pencil like I do," he realized. "We have something in common."

He stared at the back of the Little Red-Haired Girl's head, unable to focus on his test. Then he heard his teacher's voice.

"Waa waaaa waa wa," she announced.

"One minute left!" Charlie Brown said in a panic.

Charlie Brown and Peppermint Patty both looked up at the clock. Everyone else was staring at them. The two of them were the last to finish.

Charlie Brown looked at the last few questions and scribbled his answers as fast as he could. Peppermint Patty turned her answer sheet sideways and started filling in the little bubbles with her pencil. When she finished, she grinned. She had created a smiley face with her bubbles!

Charlie Brown leaped from his seat and ran up the aisle to hand in his paper. As he passed Peppermint Patty, she jumped up and raced him to the teacher's desk.

"Out of my way, Chuck!" she cried.

She grabbed ahold of him, wrestling with him until they reached the front of the room. They both reached the pile of tests at the same time and slammed down their papers. All the tests shot into the air.

"Waa waaa waa wa," said Miss Othmar.

"Write our names? Yes, ma'am," Charlie Brown said.

He reached for his paper—and his hand accidentally brushed Peppermint Patty's. She looked at him and grinned.

"Chuck, are you trying to hold my hand, you sly dog?" she asked.

A loud "ooooooh" rose up from the class.

Charlie Brown turned beet red and yanked away his hand. He jumped back, turned around, and realized he was staring at the Little Red-Haired Girl face-to-face.

"Hi, I'm Crackles," he nervously blurted out. "I mean Chuckles. I . . . ooh!"

With a scream, he ran straight out of the classroom and headed right for the nurse's office. He took a seat on the bench, sweating, puffing, and panting.

There was a little kid waiting for the nurse too, and

he took one look at Charlie Brown and slid away.

"What are you in for?" he asked.

"Have you ever had that feeling when you can't stop smiling?" Charlie Brown asked, talking a mile a minute. "You try to stand, but your knees become weak. And then that Little Red-Haired Girl glances at you and all of life's possibilities become so clear. And then you realize . . . she has no idea you're alive."

The nurse couldn't help Charlie Brown, and he knew it. For the rest of the day, he looked for a way to have a fresh start with the Little Red-Haired Girl. First impressions were important, but second impressions could make up for bad first impressions, couldn't they?

Charlie Brown got another chance on the school bus ride home. He took his usual seat, in the very last row, and plopped his pile of books next to him. Then he took the feathered pencil out of his pocket and stared at it with a sigh.

The Little Red-Haired Girl got on the bus. He saw her look around for a seat. He took a deep breath and slid his books closer to him so she would see the empty seat next to him.

In his head, he imagined how smoothly it would

go. *I'm Charlie Brown*, he would say. *I think I have your pencil. It's a really cool pencil. You know, we have something in common. I chew on my pencil too.*

But as the Little Red-Haired Girl got closer, Charlie Brown panicked. Shyness took over. Shyness, and a terrible fear of failure.

Just before she sat down, he dove under the seat in front of him. Then he crawled under the seats toward the front of the bus.

So much for smooth! Charlie Brown thought.

CHAPTER SIX
IT WAS A DARK AND STORMY NIGHT . . .

Snoopy brought the typewriter back to his doghouse. He would write the greatest novel ever written. He'd be famous! Then nobody would ever say "No dogs allowed!" to him again.

He set the typewriter on top of his doghouse and sat in front of it. Curious, Woodstock perched on top of the machine.

Snoopy put a blank piece of paper into the carriage and rolled it up, causing Woodstock to lose his balance. The little bird fell onto the keys as Snoopy began to type. Woodstock tried to get Snoopy's attention.

"Chirp! Chirp!" Woodstock complained as he dodged the metal keys. Then he flew away.

But Snoopy's friend didn't stay away for long. Woodstock landed on Snoopy's head and watched as Snoopy started typing.

Clack clackety clack! Snoopy looked at what he had written and frowned. He tore the paper out of the typewriter, crumpled it up, and tossed it into a trash can.

Clack clackety clack! Clack clackety clack! Snoopy kept typing . . . and tearing papers out of the machine. He just wasn't satisfied.

Clack clackety clack! Snoopy typed some more and then sat back. He might just have something there. . . .

Woodstock read it. Then he picked up a red pen and started marking it up. The two friends argued, and Snoopy ripped that paper out of the typewriter too and tossed it onto the pile.

Just then the sound of a tiny whirring engine filled the air. Linus's red remote-control airplane whizzed past the doghouse, sending Woodstock flying away.

Snoopy's eyes lit up as he watched the World War I plane. The scene unfolded in his mind like a movie on a screen, and he began to type. . . .

It was a dark and stormy night.

Thunder roared. Lightning
flashed in the sky. High above
the French countryside, the
World War I Flying Ace had
never been so close to his
lifelong enemy, the Red Baron!

Snoopy imagined himself as the Flying Ace, wearing a pilot's cap, goggles, and a red scarf around his neck. Seated on top of his doghouse plane, he chased after the Red Baron.

The Flying Ace zoomed toward the
red triplane, quickly catching
up. But the Red Baron looped in
the sky, evading him! Now he was
right on the Flying Ace's tail!

The Flying Ace knew he had to
escape from the Red Baron. Down
below, he saw a stone bridge

stretching over a river. If he
could reach that bridge, he
would be safe. He took a deep
breath.

The Flying Ace aimed for the
ground at superspeed. He gripped
his controls tightly. If he could
make it under the bridge, he
just might . . .

Snoopy got so excited that he actually fell off his
doghouse! *Splash!* He landed in his dog dish. He was
soaked! Woodstock laughed as Snoopy groaned.

Snoopy shook off the water and climbed back on
top of his doghouse. Inspiration had struck—and some
wet fur wasn't going to stop him!

CHAPTER SEVEN
EYE SPY

Back inside the school bus, Charlie Brown slid out from under the seats as the bus came to a stop in front of his house. Still too shy to face the Little Red-Haired Girl, he raced off the bus. He hid behind Snoopy's doghouse. After he caught his breath, he slowly peered over the top.

The Little Red-Haired Girl walked off the bus, heading to her house. Charlie Brown couldn't take his eyes off her. Curious, Snoopy stopped typing. Was this some kind of secret spy operation?

Charlie Brown cautiously snuck off toward his

house. Snoopy silently rolled off his doghouse and fol-lowed Charlie Brown.

Perched in his nest, Woodstock started to chirp quizzically. Snoopy quietly rose up behind Woodstock's nest and covered the little bird's beak, signaling for him to be quiet. Then he looked left, looked right, and ducked back down.

Charlie Brown entered his house through the back door and went to the big front window in his living room. He stepped behind the curtain and looked across the street. From there he had a perfect view of the Little Red-Haired Girl's house. As he looked through the window, Snoopy crawled across the rug. He slid under the curtains and joined Charlie Brown.

Charlie Brown watched the Little Red-Haired Girl walk down the sidewalk. She stopped at the mailbox by her front walk and checked it. Then she turned slightly toward Charlie Brown's house.

Charlie Brown felt a moment of panic. Had she seen him? But she closed the mailbox and started to walk toward her house. Suddenly, Snoopy popped out of the mailbox. He signaled to Charlie Brown. He had sighted the target!

"No!" Charlie Brown yelled, frantically waving his arms.

The Little Red-Haired Girl glanced back over her shoulder, and Charlie Brown hit the deck. He crawled out from under the curtain and raced to his bedroom.

"Whew, that was a close one," he said.

His window faced the street too, but this window had Venetian blinds. Perfect! He could see out, but nobody could see in. He twisted the blinds open a bit and watched the Little Red-Haired Girl examine her mailbox. She hadn't seen Snoopy, but she was clearly suspicious of something.

He pulled the pink pencil from his pocket and admired it. Then he gazed out the window and sighed.

"If I could only work up the nerve to go over there, I would—"

Just then the blinds flew up! Sally and Snoopy were standing in his room.

"What are you looking at, big brother?" Sally asked.

"Are you crazy?" Charlie Brown asked. Now the Little Red-Haired Girl could see him! He reached for the blinds and pulled them down. Sally grabbed the string and pulled them up.

"But I want to see what you're looking at!" Sally said.

"No!" cried Charlie Brown, pulling the blinds back down.

The brother and sister struggled to control the blinds. Charlie Brown got caught in the blinds and was pulled up and down, up and down. Snoopy's head bobbed up and down as he watched him.

Then Sally's elbow accidentally smacked into Snoopy. He went flying backward and knocked over Charlie Brown's desk lamp. The lamp shone on Charlie Brown like a spotlight. Now Charlie Brown could be seen for miles around!

Somehow, the Little Red-Haired Girl didn't notice. She walked back into her house. Sally finally saw what Charlie Brown had been looking at.

"Ohhh, you like the Little Red-Haired Girl!" she realized.

That's when it hit Snoopy. His book would not be a spy story. It would be a love story! It was just the inspiration he needed.

CHAPTER EIGHT
FIFI

Snoopy raced back to the typewriter on top of his doghouse. He ripped out the paper already in it and replaced it with a fresh sheet. He knew exactly what masterpiece he needed to write!

He furiously began to type:

Chapter One: It Was the Greatest
Story Ever Told

The Flying Ace emerged from the
airport wearing his green cap,
red scarf, and goggles. But when

he saw his plane, he gasped. He couldn't believe his eyes. This was a disaster!

The plane was in a shambles! Parts were scattered everywhere. He approached Woodstock, the leader of his flight crew. Woodstock started chirping orders to his team of mechanics—young birds loyal to the Flying Ace.

There was a flurry of action as the crew quickly fixed the plane. The Flying Ace stood behind it, inspecting it, as Woodstock turned the propeller.

POOF! A cloud of black smoke shot out, covering the Flying Ace. Woodstock glared at his team of mechanics.

The sound of an airplane engine filled the air. It was coughing and sputtering. The Flying Ace looked up to see a white plane chugging across the sky. Black smoke trailed from the tail. The plane was in trouble, and was coming down for a landing.

As it got closer, the Flying Ace saw that the plane was a White Albatross. A real beauty. The pilot flew her in for a safe, expert landing.

The Flying Ace walked toward the plane. The pilot stepped out and removed her flying cap to reveal the lovely face of a French poodle. The Flying Ace's mouth dropped.

Her name was Fifi. She was the most beautiful thing he had ever seen.

Fifi moved to the front of her plane and removed one of the panels. She pulled out a wrench and got to work fixing the engine. A smudge of grease appeared on her cheek, but the Flying Ace thought it only made her look more beautiful. She was gorgeous, and she could fix an engine!

Suddenly the Flying Ace felt
self-conscious. He rubbed most
of the grease spots (but not all)
from his own fur. Then he ran to
the grass and picked some purple
flowers. He turned to go back to
the plane, but Fifi was already
taking off again.

The Flying Ace watched in awe as
Fifi flew off toward the horizon—
right through a heart-shaped
cloud.

He was in love. But when would
he ever see her again?

CHAPTER NINE

ADVICE. 5 CENTS.

Snoopy stopped typing and sniffed the bouquet of flowers in his hand. They smelled as fresh and sweet as new love.

Woodstock took out a red pen and started marking up what Snoopy had written. Snoopy dropped the flowers on Woodstock, who chirped his objection.

Snoopy picked up another blank sheet of paper and was about to feed the typewriter when he saw Charlie Brown moping on the back stoop.

"Hmm. Maybe I should bring the Little Red-Haired Girl a housewarming gift," he said. "Snoopy, what do you think she would like? What should I bring?"

Snoopy jumped off his doghouse, holding a flower. He handed it to Charlie Brown.

"Thanks, Snoopy," Charlie Brown said. He took a deep breath and stood up. Then he began to slowly walk toward the Little Red-Haired Girl's house. Snoopy marched faithfully by his side.

"I can't believe I am about to talk to the Little Red-Haired Girl," Charlie Brown said, looking down at Snoopy. "It's moments like this when you need your faithful friend."

Charlie Brown stopped at the front door. He reached out to ring the doorbell . . . and then turned and walked away.

Snoopy pushed him back to the door.

"Yup. If there is one person you want by your side at a moment like this, it's your loyal dog," Charlie Brown repeated.

Charlie Brown reached for the doorbell . . . and then turned away again. This time Snoopy reached out and pushed the doorbell for him. Snoopy bolted!

"Aaah!" Charlie Brown wailed.

The Little Red-Haired Girl opened the door. She

looked around, but she didn't see anybody there.

"Hello? Hello?" she called out.

Nobody answered. She shrugged and closed the door.

If she had looked more closely, she would have noticed that the plant on her front stoop had legs and feet. Charlie Brown took the plant off his head and breathed a sigh of relief. Snoopy looked at him and shook his head.

Charlie Brown sighed. What was the matter with him? Why couldn't he work up the courage to talk to the Little Red-Haired Girl?

He needed advice, and he knew just where to find it. He walked over to the Van Pelt house just as the winter sun began to set overhead.

He found Lucy sitting behind a wooden booth on her lawn. The hand-painted sign in front of the roof read, PSYCHIATRIC ADVICE. 5 CENTS.

"Charlie Brown! What brings you here so late in the day?" Lucy asked.

"I need your advice on girls, Lucy," Charlie Brown said. "You're a girl, right?"

Lucy glared at him.

"Let's just say there's this girl I'd like to impress," Charlie Brown continued, "but she's something and I'm nothing. If I were something and she was nothing, I could talk to her, or if she was nothing and I was nothing, I could talk to her. But she's something and I'm nothing, so I can't just talk to her."

"That's ridiculous, Charlie Brown!" Lucy said.

"She has a pretty face, and pretty faces make me nervous," Charlie Brown explained.

"Pretty face? Pretty face?" Lucy asked, getting angrier each time she said it. "I HAVE A PRETTY FACE! HOW COME MY FACE DOESN'T MAKE YOU NERVOUS? HOW COME YOU CAN TALK TO ME, CHARLIE BROWN?"

Lucy pulled out a hand mirror and looked at her reflection. She fluffed her hair and then smiled confidently.

"I just need to know the secret to winning her heart," Charlie Brown said.

"Girls want someone with proven success," Lucy said. "Have you won any awards? Like a Congressional Medal of Honor? Or a Nobel Peace Prize?"

Charlie Brown frowned. "Uh . . ."

"What are your real estate holdings? Do you have a diversified portfolio?" Lucy asked.

Now Charlie Brown was really confused. "Huh?"

Lucy leaned forward. "Let me let you in on a little secret, Charlie Brown," she said. "If you really want to impress girls, you need to show them you're a winner!"

She pulled out a book, *10 Ways to Become a Winner!*, and handed it to Charlie Brown.

Now, this was something he could understand. "A winner? Me? Lucy, you may be on to something!"

He started flipping through the book, not listening to her.

"Of course, when I say 'you,' you know I don't mean you personally," she went on. "We all know you couldn't possibly win anything, Charlie Brown!"

Then she held out a metal cup. "That will be five cents, please!" she said, tapping loudly on the book to get his attention.

Charlie Brown dropped a coin into the cup and walked away. Lucy smiled with satisfaction, shaking her can of nickels.

"Ah! Nickels, nickels, nickels. What a beautiful sound!"

CHAPTER TEN
THE <u>TALENT SHOW</u>

The next day, Charlie Brown paced around his room reading *10 Ways to Become a Winner!*

"'Congratulations, you're on your way to becoming a winner!'" he read out loud. "'Step one: Forget everything you know about yourself.' Hmm. Okay."

That was a confusing step. If he wasn't himself, then who was he?

"'Step two. Project confidence!'" he read.

Charlie Brown put his free hand on his hip, trying to strike a confident pose. Snoopy peeked in to see what he was up to.

Charlie Brown read the next line. "'Don't slouch!'"

He straightened his back and stood as tall as he could. Snoopy jumped into the room and copied him.

"'Maintain eye contact at all times.'"

Charlie Brown looked at himself in the mirror on his dresser. Snoopy's head slowly rose up. The boy and his dog looked at each other, staring into each other's eyes.

It was a staring contest! Charlie Brown and Snoopy stared at each other intensely. Their eyes began to water. Finally, Charlie Brown blinked, and Snoopy did a victory dance.

Then they both heard a loud crashing noise from the living room and rushed to investigate it. There they found the room filled with cardboard boxes painted to look like rodeo barrels. Sally was dressed as a rodeo rider and held a lasso in her hand. She rode a horse made from a mop with a paper bag for a nose.

"Giddyap, little pony! Yee-haw!" Sally cried.

"What are you doing?" Charlie Brown asked.

"I'm going to be a rodeo star in the school talent show!" she announced. She started twirling her lasso, and then she began to talk like a cowboy. "Why, when

I win that first prize ribbon, there will be no one who hasn't heard the name Sally Brown, and her trusted horse, Target!"

She tossed the lasso at Charlie Brown. It landed on his head and shoulders and then loosely fell to the floor. Then Sally jumped on Snoopy's back and rode out of the living room with a triumphant "Yee-haw!"

Charlie Brown's eyes lit up. "Win the talent show. Now, that's a great idea! That's just the sort of thing Lucy was talking about!"

Charlie Brown didn't have much time to get an act together, but Snoopy helped him. Over the next few nights, they worked on some homemade magic tricks. Charlie Brown had seen lots of magicians on TV. It couldn't be that hard, could it?

Things didn't start out so smoothly. He began by putting a pile of fruit on the kitchen table. Then he pulled out the tablecloth. In a perfect trick, the fruit would stay exactly where it was.

"Ta-da!" Charlie Brown said.

But when Charlie Brown tried it, all the fruit rolled to the floor.

But the failed trick didn't discourage him. He

and Snoopy worked hard on their act. They made a disappearing box, a levitation box, and even a body-switching box—all out of cardboard.

When the night of the talent show arrived, Charlie Brown was nervous and excited at the same time. Backstage, he got his tricks ready as the house lights went down and the stage lights went up. Everyone in the audience hushed—including the Little Red-Haired Girl.

The show opened with Schroeder, who played a piece by Beethoven on his piano.

Backstage, Charlie Brown's friends saw him pushing in a cart carrying his homemade tricks. They looked pretty impressive—and so did Charlie Brown. He wore a spiffy tuxedo and a tall top hat.

"Whoa, look at that," said Frieda.

"That can't be Charlie Brown, can it?" asked Patty.

"Wow!" said Shermy.

Charlie Brown took off his hat and handed it to Snoopy. Then he walked to the curtain and peeked out at the crowd. There, in the third row, sat the Little Red-Haired Girl.

"She's here," Charlie Brown said. "I have a really

good feeling that tonight she will see the new Charlie Brown."

"Charlie Brown," a voice repeated, and a spotlight clicked on backstage, illuminating Lucy.

"Charlie Brown," she said. "I'm surprised to see you here. After a lifetime of failure, I—"

Lucy looked to her right and saw a shadow imitating her. It was Snoopy!

"Ugh, I ought to slug you!" Lucy cried.

She swung at Snoopy, who ducked. Then he licked Lucy's face. Lucy shrieked and started to run in circles.

"Ugh! I've been kissed by a dog! I have dog germs! Get hot water! Get some disinfectant! Get some iodine!"

One by one the acts took the stage. Franklin rushed around, organizing the performers.

"Let's keep this thing moving, time's a-wasting!" he urged.

The audience applauded for each act. A nervous Marcie held wooden boards while Peppermint Patty karate chopped them. Then it was Sally's turn. She was all dressed up in her rodeo costume, holding her homemade mop horse. The stage crew worked quickly to set up her boxes painted to look like rodeo barrels.

"Okay, Sally, you're up," Franklin told her. "We're running behind, so get a move on."

Sally nodded and galloped forward as the curtain opened.

"Giddyap, little pony!" she cried. "Yee-haw!"

Sally leaped onto the stage as Western music played in the background. "Ride 'em cowgirl!" she cheered, twirling her lasso.

Some people in the crowd laughed nervously at her silly excuse for a horse. That made Sally nervous. She tossed the lasso over a cardboard cow, and it fell over with a thud.

The crowd laughed again, and then they went silent. Poor Sally was so embarrassed! She stopped galloping, and the paper bag nose of her horse slid off.

Sally froze, mortified. She stared out at the crowd. The music stopped. An uncomfortable silence filled the auditorium.

Charlie Brown was busy setting up his magic boxes when Franklin pulled him aside.

"Your sister is really dying out there," Franklin informed him.

The boys peeked onstage, and Charlie Brown frowned. His sister wasn't even moving.

"Sorry, Charlie Brown, this has gone on long enough," Franklin said. He called to the stage crew. "Drop the curtain!"

Charlie Brown held up his hand. "Don't do that! She hasn't finished her act yet."

"Well, it's either her act or yours," Franklin said. "We can't let this go on forever."

Charlie Brown looked onstage again. Sally had tears in her eyes now. He knew what he had to do. He looked down at Snoopy.

"Come on, Snoopy. We've got to help Sally," he said.

Charlie Brown moved to the table he had set up with a tablecloth and a tower of fruit. Without even thinking, he pulled off the tablecloth. Not a single piece of fruit moved!

Charlie Brown walked off. A minute later, he appeared onstage.

"Moo!" he said.

Charlie Brown had worked quickly to make a cow costume. He had cut holes in his tux to look like the patterns of a cow. He'd used the tablecloth to make horns and a tail.

The crowd started to laugh. Everyone craned his or her neck to get a better look. The Little Red-Hair Girl eyed him curiously.

"Big brother? What are you doing?" Sally whispered frantically.

"Rope me!" Charlie Brown hissed back. "Moo!"

Snoopy bounded onstage wearing a bridle and saddle. Sally jumped onto his back. In her excitement, she grabbed Snoopy's ears like they were reins and pulled back hard. He let out a wild shriek.

Then Sally galloped across the stage, riding Snoopy and chasing Charlie Brown!

"I'm gonna get you!" she cried.

Sally chased Charlie Brown all over the stage. The crowd loved it! Sally got caught up in the excitement. She rode Snoopy like a crazed cowgirl on a wild stallion.

Charlie Brown ran backstage to escape her, but Sally followed him. Franklin dove out of the way, grabbing the rope to the backstage curtain as he fell. The curtain pulled up, revealing all of the backstage performers.

Sally and Charlie Brown crashed through them all, knocking over microphone stands and props. The performers fled, screaming. They almost trampled Peppermint Patty, but Marcie quickly grabbed her by the arm and judo flipped her out of the way.

"Sorry, sir," Marcie said.

But Peppermint Patty was impressed. "Good one!"

Lucy was too busy leaning on Schroeder's piano and gazing into his eyes to notice the commotion. But Schroder saw the cow and cowgirl coming and swiftly yanked his piano out of harm's way, knocking over Lucy.

"You can run, little doggie, but you can't hide!" Sally called to Charlie Brown.

Franklin leaped out of her way, pulling the back-stage curtain back down with him. Now Charlie Brown was back onstage, with Sally still chasing him on Snoopy.

She tossed the lasso and it landed around his chest. He flew up, then crashed down to the stage. Sally got off Snoopy and ran to Charlie Brown. She picked him up like a rodeo rider holding a calf, tossed him onto his side, and wrapped the rope around him.

"My name is Calamity Sally, the best bronco-busting, lasso-roping cowgirl in this here town!" she announced.

The crowd went wild! Sally leaned over to Charlie Brown and whispered in his ear.

"Thanks, big brother," she said.

Lightbulbs flashed as everyone took pictures of Charlie Brown, all tied up in his silly cow costume.

Charlie Brown groaned. This was *not* the way he wanted to get famous!

CHAPTER ELEVEN
SHE LIKES TO DANCE!

The next day at school Charlie Brown's photo was plastered on the front of the school newspaper. The headline read, *Moo!*

"Good grief," Charlie Brown said with a sigh as he saw the stack of newspapers by the lunchroom entrance. "It's not really that bad, is it? Nobody reads the school paper anyhow."

Charlie Brown walked into the cafeteria. Every single student was reading a newspaper! They all looked up at him.

"Moo!" they said loudly.

Embarrassed, Charlie Brown walked over to Linus.

"Look on the bright side, Charlie Brown," Linus said. "At least you made the front page."

"Is there any chance that the Little Red-Haired Girl doesn't read the school paper?" Charlie Brown wondered hopefully.

The boys sat at their usual table and took out their lunches.

"Peanut butter again," Charlie Brown reported as he unwrapped his sandwich. Then he spied the Little Red-Haired Girl across the room. He stared at her.

"You know, Charlie Brown, if you like her so much, why not just walk up to her and introduce yourself?" Linus asked.

"After the complete fool I made out of myself last night?" Charlie Brown replied. "Yeah, and why don't I just fly to the moon!"

Linus bit into his sandwich while Charlie Brown continued to stare at the Little Red-Haired Girl. He watched as Violet, Patty, and Lucy joined her at the table and they began talking.

Oh, brother, they're talking to her? Charlie Brown thought. *So much for a fresh start. Time is running out!*

As soon as he got home from school, Charlie Brown picked up *10 Ways to Become a Winner!* and began pacing around his living room, reading out loud.

"'Number six: Tell yourself, "I am worthy. I can do this. I have what it takes."'"

The phone rang, and Sally darted over to it and answered it.

"Hello?" she asked, and then she grinned and held out the receiver to Charlie Brown. "Your girlfriend's on the phone."

Charlie Brown jumped up, panicked. The book flew out of his hands. He took a deep breath and slowly approached the phone. The Little Red-Haired Girl was calling him! He could do this! He just had to stay cool.

Sally rolled her eyes as she handed him the phone and then walked away. Charlie Brown stretched the long telephone cord as far away from Sally's listening ears as he could. Then he froze, unable to speak. After an uncomfortable silence, a familiar voice came from the other end.

"Hey, Chuck!"

It was Peppermint Patty! Charlie Brown let out his breath. At least it wasn't stressful talking to Peppermint

Patty. They'd been friends for a long time.

"How've you been?" she asked him.

"Well, I—" Charlie Brown began.

Peppermint Patty was talking a mile a minute. Charlie Brown nervously paced around as she talked, tangling himself in the phone cord.

"Listen, I have some great news for you, Chuck," she was saying. "The Winter Dance is coming up and Marcie put me in charge of the refreshment committee. I took it upon myself and signed you up to make the cupcakes."

"You did what?" Charlie Brown asked. "I can't make cupcakes. The only thing I *do* know how to make is toast. Besides, why would I even want to go to the Winter Dance?"

Peppermint Patty ignored his question. "Toast and cupcakes. That sounds good, Chuck. See you there!"

"Hold on! I said—" But Peppermint Patty had already hung up.

Charlie Brown looked down at himself. He was all tangled up in the cord! He slowly unraveled himself. Toast and cupcakes? How had he gotten himself into that?

After dinner he was still wondering how to get out of that mess as he brought a stack of newspapers to the curb for recycling. A light snow was gently falling from the moonlit sky. As he put down the newspapers, he heard faint music coming from across the street.

A warm, glowing light came from the house of the Little Red-Haired Girl. Through the picture window in the front, he could see her gracefully dancing around her living room. To Charlie Brown, she looked just like an angel inside a snow globe.

An idea struck Charlie Brown. He raced back into his house, into his bedroom, and shut the door.

A few minutes later Sally was in the living room, building a house made of playing cards. Snoopy watched her. She had already built the first floor and was very carefully placing cards on top to make the second.

Suddenly, she heard a noise.

Thump. Thump. Thump.

Then the floor and walls began to shake. Her card house toppled over.

"Hey! What's going on?" she called out.

The loud music was coming from Charlie Brown's

room, right next to the living room. She began to pound her fist against the wall.

"Turn it down! Turn it down in there!"

But the music just got louder. Sally angrily walked down the hall toward Charlie Brown's bedroom. Snoopy followed her. She flung open the door.

Charlie Brown was dancing in the middle of his room, holding a mop for his dance partner. He was hopping around and flailing his arms like crazy.

Crash! He knocked a lamp right off his nightstand.

Sally was stunned.

"She likes to dance!" Charlie Brown cried as he jumped into the air.

Sally sighed, turned, and walked away. Snoopy, however, knew he had to help. He tore the mop out of Charlie Brown's hands. Then he snapped his fingers, and the lights went dark. When the lights came on again, they were shining on Snoopy, who was wearing the cape of a Spanish dancer.

He danced a circle around Charlie Brown, expertly twirling and tapping his feet on the floor. When he finished, he motioned to Charlie Brown to copy him.

Charlie Brown jumped around and waved his arms.

Snoopy put a mortified paw to his face. The boy was hopeless! Then he marched out of the room.

When he returned, he was carrying a box marked DANCE KIT. Charlie Brown watched as Snoopy pulled cutouts of footprints from the box and placed them on the floor. Each footprint had a number on it. He placed them in a simple square pattern, then nodded to Charlie Brown.

Charlie Brown stepped on the numbered footprints.

"1-2-3-4, 1-2-3-4, 1-2-3-4," he chanted as he practiced, and Snoopy nodded his approval.

For the next few days Charlie Brown had dance fever. He practiced his steps as he brushed his teeth. He moved his feet as he sat at his desk in school. He danced in the living room as Sally watched TV.

"You know, I could really use a dance partner," Charlie Brown said. Sally was not interested.

"Not on your life!" she said.

Charlie Brown retreated to his bedroom with Snoopy.

"Okay, Snoopy, I got the basics down," Charlie Brown told him. "But if I'm going to win, I need to step it up."

Snoopy laid out more footprints on the floor. This time he used more footprints and the pattern was more complicated. Charlie Brown studied it for a minute and then began to dance.

He was flawless! Perfect! Snoopy applauded.

Charlie Brown grinned and started to daydream.

"I can see it now . . . ," he said.

He performed his dance perfectly on the dance floor. So did the Little Red-Haired Girl.

"We have our winners!" Franklin said. "And now let us begin our traditional dance of the champions."

Charlie Brown extended a hand to the Little Red-Haired Girl, and she took it. They began to dance, and everyone gathered around them, cheering them on. As the music swelled, Charlie Brown dipped the Little Red-Haired Girl. He gazed into her furry face. . . .

Furry face? Charlie Brown snapped out of his daydream when he realized that he was dipping Snoopy. The dog leaned in and kissed Charlie Brown's cheek.

"Snoopy!" Charlie Brown cried, laughing. "Thanks for your help. I left some cookies in your dog dish."

Snoopy raced out of the room, slamming the door behind him. It created a gust of wind, scattering the footprints all over the bedroom floor. Now the steps were completely different.

Charlie Brown turned back to the footprints. He didn't realize that they had changed.

"Now, to practice," he said. "The dance is tomorrow night!"

CHAPTER TWELVE
THE BIG DANCE

The next night, kids swarmed into the school gym for the big dance. Balloons covered the ceiling, paper streamers were hung high above, and colored lights cast their glow on the walls as a mirror ball spun in the center of the gym. One of the kids was a DJ, spinning records in the corner.

The boys all headed to one side of the room, and the girls all stayed together on the other side. Patty looked across the dance floor at Pigpen, who was dancing confidently by himself.

"You know, I've always wanted to dance with

Pigpen," she whispered to Violet. Violet was shocked.

A large dust cloud was forming around Pigpen as he danced. Violet looked at Patty like she had lost her mind.

"Uh, yuck!" Violet said.

But even Pigpen was too shy to step into the middle of the dance floor. Sally looked around with frustration.

"Why isn't anyone dancing? It's called a dance!" she complained. Then she spotted Linus across the room. As she walked toward him, he hid himself under his blanket.

"Someone needs to get this dance started," Sally said. She grabbed Linus and pulled him out to the dance floor.

Linus wouldn't dance. So Sally wrapped his blanket around him and pulled on it, making him dance with her.

Sally and Linus broke the ice. The other kids streamed onto the dance floor and broke out their best moves.

Outside, Charlie Brown made his way to the gym, carrying a tray of cupcakes. He couldn't wait to show off his new dance moves. And that wasn't all.

"These cupcakes don't look half-bad, if I do say so myself," he told Snoopy.

He didn't notice Snoopy grab a cupcake with a quick swipe of his paw. Then he gobbled it up. Delicious! Snoopy greedily eyed the other cupcakes.

"This time I've come totally prepared," Charlie Brown said proudly. "I couldn't have done it without you, Snoopy."

Chomp! Chomp! Chomp! Snoopy ate another cupcake . . . and another . . . and another . . .

"The old Charlie Brown would still be lying in bed with a stomachache," he went on.

He stopped in front of the school doors. This was it! Then he looked down at the tray and saw that it was empty. He turned back to Snoopy and saw the dog with an innocent look on his face—and lots of frosting, too!

Charlie Brown chuckled. "Good grief!"

Charlie Brown stepped into the gym. Peppermint Patty and Marcie entered right behind him. They each held one side of a large punch bowl filled with punch.

Peppermint Patty's eyes got wide when she saw the scene inside.

"Marcie, look! Everyone's here!" she cried, and then she dropped her side of the punch bowl and ran onto the dance floor.

Marcie staggered backward with the heavy punch bowl, almost dropping it! Charlie Brown came to her rescue.

"Let me help you with that, Marcie," he said, taking the bowl from her.

Marcie smiled. "You're such a gentleman, Charles," she said, and then she joined Peppermint Patty.

Charlie Brown looked around the gym, nervously scouting it out. Then he spotted the Little Red-Haired Girl on the dance floor with Patty, Violet, and Lucy.

"She's here!" he said happily.

But as he moved into the gym, the door shut behind him, catching his shirt. He couldn't move, and he couldn't put down the punch bowl to free his shirt. He was stuck!

Then the music died down and Franklin moved to the center of the room, holding a microphone.

"Okay, ladies. It's time for you to show off your best moves. Who will win the first half of our dance competition and take home the trophy?" he asked.

The music kicked back in and the girls formed two lines on the dance floor, creating an aisle between them. One by one, the girls danced down the aisle.

Charlie Brown struggled to see the dancing. He knew the Little Red-Haired Girl was good. She had to win, so that when he won the boys' dance they would get to dance together!

When it was the Little Red-Haired Girl's turn to dance, all he could see was her red hair bopping up and down above the line of dancers. But everybody applauded loudly for her. Charlie Brown was hopeful.

"Listen to that noise," Franklin said. "I think it's safe to say we know who our winner is!"

Charlie Brown smiled as the Little Red-Haired Girl accepted her trophy.

"And now it's the gentlemen's turn to see who will be joining our lovely winning lady for the final dance of the night," Franklin said.

The boys began to line up, and Charlie Brown started to panic. He tried to pull away from the door, but he was still stuck! The music started again, and Charlie Brown leaned forward as hard as he could to try to get free.

Then . . . *bam!* Snoopy burst through the door, wearing sunglasses and a shirt that read JOE COOL. Charlie Brown rocketed forward, still holding the punch bowl.

Charlie Brown struggled to keep the punch from spilling out, but it was no use. Punch splashed out as he carried it as fast as he could to the refreshment table. When he finally slid the bowl onto the table, it was nearly empty.

But at least he was free! He looked down at his hand, where he had written down his dance steps in ink. The punch had washed them off. Charlie Brown frowned—but it wasn't the end of the world. He had practiced hard.

"This is it," he told himself. "It's now or never."

He joined the line of dancers. Patty and Violet looked at him and started laughing.

Charlie Brown's confidence deflated. He started letting other boys go in front of him.

One by one, the boys danced down the aisle. Snoopy took his turn, busting out his best dance moves.

"Whoa!" cried Peppermint Patty. "Check out the moves on that funny-looking kid with the big nose."

Then Snoopy noticed Charlie Brown. He danced over to a light pointed at the ceiling and aimed it at Charlie Brown.

Charlie Brown couldn't hide. He took a deep breath.

"Okay, just like you practiced," he told himself. "Remember the steps."

Charlie Brown danced his way down the aisle.

1-2-3-4, he chanted in his head. He remembered the dance!

The crowd started to slowly clap. Charlie Brown gained confidence. He took things up a notch, adding fancy twirls and fast foot moves. He was graceful. He was skilled. He was fabulous!

"Charlie Brown?" Frieda asked in wonder.

"All right!" cheered Shermy.

"It looks like we might have a winner here!" Franklin said as everyone clapped and cheered for Charlie Brown.

It's going to happen! I'm going to dance with the Little Red-Haired Girl! he thought.

Then he took his final dance step—and slipped in the spilled punch! His shoe flew off his foot and hit the fire sprinkler overhead. Water rained down on everyone!

All the kids ran out of the gym. It washed the dirt right off Pigpen. He looked like a completely different kid. Patty stared at him in confusion.

"Do I know you?" Patty asked.

Charlie Brown sadly watched everyone leave.

"Where's everybody going?" he yelled after them. "It's not over yet!"

He was supposed to win the dance contest. He was supposed to dance with the Little Red-Haired Girl. . . .

A stream of water rained down on his head. As Snoopy came over and opened an umbrella to protect him from the water, Charlie Brown sighed and said, "This isn't how it was supposed to end!"

CHAPTER THIRTEEN
LOST FOREVER

Water dripped from Charlie Brown as he walked down the sidewalk with Snoopy. The full moon shone brightly above them. There was a faint buzzing in the background as the red remote-control plane zipped across the sky.

Charlie Brown stopped by Snoopy's doghouse, where Woodstock waited for them, perched in a tree branch.

"I hate to say it, Snoopy, but I may have lost her forever," Charlie Brown said sadly.

Snoopy put a hand on Charlie Brown's back. Then

he handed him a cupcake, but Charlie Brown wasn't interested. He headed inside the house with his head hanging low.

Moved by Charlie Brown's emotions, Snoopy hopped up onto his doghouse and began to type.

```
The Flying Ace took to the air,
in search of his long-lost love,
Fifi.


He flew across the sky, keeping
his eyes peeled for her white
plane. Finally, he spotted
her! Fifi, piloting her White
Albatross, was flying right
toward him. Her eyes widened
when she saw him.


The Flying Ace steered his plane
next to Fifi's. She looked over at
him and smiled. He did a loop in
the sky to impress her. When he
finished, Fifi steered her plane
into a DOUBLE loop.


Then she took off in front of the
Flying Ace, and he followed her.
The two planes looped and dipped
```

in the sky. Then they both
dropped down and flew across a
green valley below.

Fifi held up a camera and
started snapping photos of the
Flying Ace in his plane. He
hammed it up, striking poses for
her—which is why he didn't see
the old barn up ahead.

WHOOSH! The Flying Ace zipped
through the barn and came out
on the other side covered in hay.
He flashed an embarrassed smile
at Fifi, and she smiled back.

Fifi steered up and grabbed a
piece of cloud with her hand.
Then she blew on it, and it
formed the shape of a heart. It
floated across the sky toward
the Flying Ace.

He responded by rolling his
plane above the valley. When the
plane was upright again, the
Flying Ace held flowers in his
hand. He flew up next to Fifi
and extended them toward her.

BOOM! The flowers exploded!
Startled, Fifi and the Flying
Ace looked behind them.

A red plane circled them and
then flew across their path. The
Red Baron!

He flew off into the distance,
but the Flying Ace gave chase.

Then the Red Baron set his
sights on Fifi's plane.

He steered right on top of the
White Albatross. Then he dipped
down and punctured her wing
with his wheel. Fifi's damaged
plane suddenly rolled over!

Taken by surprise, Fifi fell
out of the cockpit! The Flying
Ace dove down with a shriek,
determined to save her.

Just before he reached her,
Fifi pulled the string on her
parachute. She shot up in the
air as the chute blew open.

The Flying Ace banked hard,
flying straight up to try to
reach Fifi. As she slowly began
to float back toward the ground,
the Red Baron zoomed toward her.

Both pilots raced toward Fifi. At
the last second the Red Baron's
wing snagged the string of the
parachute. Then he flew off,
with Fifi dangling from his
wing!

The Flying Ace flew as fast as he
could toward the Red Baron. The
villain headed toward a large
mountain. A long bridge with
train tracks led into a dark
tunnel inside the mountain. A
train was chugging across the
bridge, headed for the tunnel.

ZOOM! The Red Baron zipped
inside the tunnel just before
the train. The Flying Ace
followed him.

Then Fifi's pink scarf flew out
of the tunnel, covering the face
of the Flying Ace! He ripped it

```
off, but he was too late. The
craggy face of the mountain was
quickly approaching . . .
```

Riiiiiip! Woodstock tore the paper out of the type-writer. Snoopy's hands covered his face as he trembled in fear. He slowly removed his hands to see Woodstock looking at him.

Grateful to his friend for saving him, he took the paper from Woodstock and read over the last line he had typed.

```
He thought he had lost her
forever.
```

CHAPTER FOURTEEN
A PERFECT SCORE?

As Charlie Brown walked into his classroom the next day, he noticed that the Little Red-Haired Girl's desk was empty. Was she late?

He sat at his desk and stared at hers, wishing for her to appear.

"You can quit daydreaming, Charlie Brown," Linus said. "She's not here."

"Daydreaming? Me?" Charlie Brown asked innocently. Then he blushed.

"She'll be back Monday," Linus explained. "I heard she went back east to help take care of her grandmother, who isn't feeling well. I thought that was nice of her."

"She seems like the kind of person who would do that sort of thing," Charlie Brown mused.

"Waa wa waa waaa wa," said Miss Othmar as class began.

"Aww! Not another book report!" someone moaned.

"Waa wa waa," Miss Othmar went on.

"Time to pick our partners," said Linus.

The teacher called Violet to the front of the room first. Violet reached into a paper bag and pulled out a slip of paper.

She looked at the name. "Patty!"

"Yes! All right!" Patty cheered.

The two girls mimed high-fiving each other as Violet returned to her seat. Then it was Lucy's turn. She picked a name from the bag and looked at it.

"Nope," she said. Then picked another one. "Not this one."

She kept going until she found the name she was looking for.

"Schroeder!" she cried happily, gazing at him. "There's no denying it. It was meant to be."

Schroeder put his head in his heads.

"*Waa wa waaa,*" said Miss Othmar.

Charlie Brown walked to the front of the class. He cast a hopeful glance at the Little Red-Haired Girl's desk. Would he be lucky enough to pick her name? He imagined the two of them getting their book report back from Miss Othmar with a gold star on it—the prize for the best book report in the class. The Little Red-Haired Girl would be so impressed with him!

Charlie Brown stuck his hand into the bag. Then he pulled it out and read the name. A huge grin spread across his face!

"The Little Red-Haired Girl," he said quietly to himself. "My lucky day!"

But as Charlie Brown walked back to his desk, the reality sank in. He and the Little Red-Haired Girl would be working together. Side by side. Talking.

By the time the lunch bell rang, he was in a panic. He grabbed Linus's shirt and shook him in the hallway. Then the words spilled out of him.

"You've got to help me, Linus! I'm not sure I can handle being partners with the Little Red-Haired Girl. I need to slow things down. Maybe I'm not ready for a serious relationship. How will I support her? I can't afford a mortgage. What if I'm put into escrow?"

"Charlie Brown, you're being ridiculous," Linus told him, breaking away from his friend. "You haven't said one word to her, and you're already married with a house payment?"

"I've never been responsible for anything before," he said. "This could be the worst thing that ever happened to her!"

They entered the cafeteria and headed toward their table. Charlie Brown took the pink pencil from his pocket and stared at it.

Suddenly, he had a flash of inspiration.

"Linus, it just hit me," he said. "I think I know how to become her hero! While she's away helping her grandmother, I could complete the book report for the two of us."

"That's one way to go," Linus said. "But if you want my advice—"

Suddenly, the other kids began to stream out of the cafeteria.

"Where is everyone going?" Linus wondered out loud.

"They're posting the test scores! Come on!" someone yelled.

Charlie Brown and Linus followed the crowd. A
group of kids had gathered in front of a display case in
the hallway.

"Look! Someone got a perfect score, sir," Marcie
told Peppermint Patty.

"You would have to be a genius to get a perfect
score," her friend replied.

"I didn't even know that was possible," said Violet.

There was a gasp as the kids in front read the
name of the kid who had the highest score. As Charlie
Brown approached with Linus, kids turned to stare at
him.

"It's him!" cried Patty.

"Here he comes," said Violet.

"No one in the world has ever gotten a hundred
before," Patty added.

The crowd parted for Charlie Brown. He stepped
up to the glass case, confused. He started at the bottom of the list, searching for his name. But it wasn't
on the bottom. He scrolled all the way up to the top.

He stared at his name at the top of the list, stunned.

"A perfect score? Me? This can't be right," he said.

"No, Charlie Brown, look. You really *do* have a perfect score," Linus pointed out.

"Huh," said Charlie Brown, still stunned. He would never have believed it, but there it was, on the list, right in front of his eyes. "I have heard peanut butter is brain food."

Peppermint Patty slapped him on the back. "Nice job, Chuck ol' boy."

"I always knew you had it in you, Charles," said Marcie.

Lucy's voice came from the back of the crowd.

"This can't be right! Out of my way!"

She pushed her way through the kids and stopped in front of Charlie Brown. "Mr. Perfect: Charlie Brown? It must be a typo! I don't believe it. I won't believe it!"

She stormed off, enraged. Then a voice came over the speakers.

"Good afternoon, students and staff," said Franklin. "We have a special announcement. There will be an all-school assembly on Monday morning to celebrate our illustrious classmate, Charlie Brown, who achieved a perfect score on the standardized test."

Everyone stared at Charlie Brown in shock. Then they burst into cheers. A kid came up and grabbed Charlie Brown's books for him. Then a bunch of kids escorted him down the hallway.

"Make way! Genius coming through!" Peppermint Patty yelled.

CHAPTER FIFTEEN

CHARLIE BROWN, GENIUS

Kids treated Charlie Brown like a celebrity as he walked down the hallway.

"I have a science project due next week," said Franklin. "Can you give me your thoughts?"

"Hey, I saw him first!" complained Shermy.

Charlie Brown's next class was art, where he was supposed to be making a sculpture out of wire coat hangers. He looked around at the other kids. Schroeder had made a perfect piano. Shermy's looked like a cool dinosaur.

Charlie Brown bent and twisted the coat hangers,

quickly ending up with a mess. Franklin spotted it.

"Will you look at this," he said. "What a contemporary piece."

A group of kids gathered around.

"Nice use of space," said Patty.

Lucy looked at the mess at Charlie Brown's workstation and rolled her eyes. "Have you all lost your minds?"

Charlie Brown was still famous when school ended. After the last bell, the kids all went to the ice pond for a game of hockey. Charlie Brown got control of the puck and skated toward the goal.

"Shoot it, Charlie Brown! Shoot it!" Franklin yelled.

Charlie Brown hit the puck. It veered off course, flying off the pond and bouncing off a tree trunk. Then it zoomed back to the pond toward the goal, where Marcie was guarding the net. Her goalie pads were bigger than she was, and her glasses were fogged up from the cold.

Peppermint Patty quickly skated in front of her to try to intercept the puck, but she missed. Marcie could barely move, and the puck glided past her through the net. Marcie was impressed.

"Nice use of angles there, Charles," said Marcie.

Charlie Brown's teammates crowded around him, cheering. Lucy kept her distance.

Something was wrong here, she thought. She knew that Charlie Brown wasn't a genius. But how could she prove it?

Charlie Brown's fans escorted him to his house, and he waved good-bye to them at his front door. Except for the Little Red-Haired Girl not being there, this had been the best day of his life!

His little sister, Sally, was happy for her big brother—and she knew just how to latch on to his fame. Early the next morning, before school, she led a group of Charlie Brown's biggest fans—Peppermint Patty, Marcie, and some little kids from her class— through a tour of the Browns' house.

"And this is where it all began," she said, point- ing to a living room chair. "As a youth he passed many hours just sitting in that chair, keeping his deep thoughts to himself."

Next she led them to a closet. When she opened it, a bunch of broken kites fell out.

"And here we have his early kites, used in many

THE DOCTOR

aerodynamic studies," she said, pointing at the broken kites.

"Whoa!" The group of kids was impressed.

Then Sally led them to Charlie Brown's bedroom door.

"If we are lucky, we will see him in his natural habitat," she whispered.

She slowly opened his door and led the group inside. They surrounded Charlie Brown's bed.

"And this is the actual bed where he lies and ponders life's greatest questions," Sally said.

Charlie Brown woke up to see a crowd of kids staring at him.

"Hey! What are you doing?" he cried.

"I'm trying to cash in on your celebrity," Sally explained.

Charlie Brown shooed them out and managed to eat his breakfast in peace. But another throng of kids waited for him at his bus stop. He needed Snoopy and Woodstock to safely escort him onto the bus, wearing Secret Service uniforms.

The whole school day was a crazy blur. Lots of kids were wearing yellow shirts with black zigzags, just like

Charlie Brown. Everyone kept asking him for advice. He was more popular than he had ever dreamed!

At the end of the day, he and Linus left the school.

"I haven't seen you in a while," Linus said.

"I've been so busy lately, I keep getting pulled in all sorts of directions," Charlie Brown explained. "Even my little sister is treating me like I'm some sort of celebrity."

Just as he said it, a bunch of kids swarmed out of the school.

"There he is!" someone shouted.

They crowded around him. Frieda grabbed his right arm. "Charlie Brown, let's go sledding!"

Franklin grabbed his left arm. "Come help us with our snow castle!"

Sally pushed her way through the crowd, accompanied by a kid carrying a camera and another with a microphone.

"This will make a great documentary," she said. "Action!"

Pigpen pushed past Franklin. "Do you have time to help me with my book report?" he asked. "It's due on Monday."

Charlie Brown's heart sank.

"Monday? The report is due on Monday?" he asked. That was just a few days away! "She's back on Monday! I haven't even started yet."

He was in trouble. But he knew who could help him.

"Does anybody know where Marcie is?" he asked.

"She went skating with Peppermint Patty," Schroeder replied.

Charlie Brown ran off toward the ice pond.

"Cut!" Sally yelled.

CHAPTER SIXTEEN
THE LONGEST BOOK EVER

Over at the ice pond, Marcie sat on a bench, freezing, as Peppermint Patty shot pucks across the ice.

"Please just pick one book for your report, sir," Marcie pleaded, looking down at the paper in her hands. "I made this list of the greatest books of all time just for you."

"Ah, let me sleep on it, Marcie," Peppermint Patty said, shooting another puck.

Frustrated, Marcie got up and walked away. A minute later Charlie Brown walked up to the pond.

"I'm looking for Marcie," he told Peppermint

Patty. "I need her to help me find the greatest book of all time."

Peppermint Patty skidded to a stop. "I just might be able to help you there, Chuck. Marcie just read off a long list of great novels. *Huckleberry* something, *Catcher with a Pie*. But she said the greatest book of all time is *Leo's Toy Store* by some guy called Warren Peace."

"*Leo's Toy Store*," he repeated thoughtfully.

"Yup! That's the one, Chuck!" she said, and then skated away.

Charlie Brown thanked Peppermint Patty and went to the library. He started off in the children's section. He went to the *L*s and started pulling out books one by one.

"Nope. None of them are *Leo's Toy Store*," he said with a sigh. He walked away, leaving a tower of books behind him. That could only mean one thing.

The book must be in the grown-up section. He headed there and found the fiction shelves. What had Peppermint Patty said the author's name was, again? Warren Peace? He found his way to the *P*s and took two books off the shelf. Behind them, he saw Marcie on the other side of the shelf.

"Charles? I've never seen you in here before," she said, surprised.

"Marcie, can you help me find a copy of *Leo's Toy Store*?" he asked. "Peppermint Patty told me you said it was the greatest—"

Marcie shook her head. "Stop right there, Charles. Come with me."

She led him down another aisle of books and stopped, looking up. At the very top was a massive book, covered in dust.

"That's what you're looking for," she said. "*War and Peace* by Leo Tolstoy."

Charlie Brown climbed a ladder and looked at the book in disbelief.

"Yikes! How long was this war?" he asked.

"Are you sure that is the book you want to read?" she asked. "Might I remind you, Charles, you only have the weekend to complete your report."

"I have to if I'm going to win that gold star," he said.

He tried to pull the book off the shelf, but it was stuck. He yanked with all his might. The bookshelf began to wobble.

Suddenly, the book broke free, sending Charlie Brown flying backward. He fell to the floor, still clutching *War and Peace* as a waterfall of books tumbled down and landed on top of him.

"Charles!" Marcie wailed. She helped Charlie Brown out of the pile of books. Getting the 1,225-page copy of *War and Peace* out of the library wasn't going to be easy, but Charlie Brown was determined. Snoopy and Woodstock came to help him.

First, they pushed the book down the library steps. It fell right at the feet of Lucy.

"Big book. How are you going to get it home, smarty-pants?" she asked.

Charlie Brown pulled up a wooden sled. He opened up the book and flipped it over onto the sled.

"Pretty smart," Lucy said as Charlie Brown pulled the sled away, and then she slapped her hand over her mouth. No! She was not going to become one of Charlie Brown's fans.

Charlie Brown pulled the sled down the street. He came to the top of a hill, and the sled pulled away from him. He quickly jumped on it as the sled slid down the hill, over bumps and dips in the street. Snoopy came sledding down next to him, riding his dog dish.

Bump! The sled lurched, and the book slid off! Charlie Brown reached out to grab it, but the book was just out of reach.

Bump! The sled hit the bottom of the hill and soared, landing on a frozen river. So did the book! Charlie Brown zipped across the ice at super speed, but he still couldn't reach the book.

Zoom! Charlie Brown launched off the frozen river and into his neighborhood. He came to a slow stop in his backyard. Behind him, the book shot across the snowy lawn like a freight train.

Bam! The book hit Charlie Brown, and they both went flying into his house.

It was Friday afternoon. Charlie Brown had until Monday to read the book and write the report. As soon as he finished dinner, he sat in a comfy chair and slammed the book open on a table in front of him.

"'War and Peace,'" he read aloud. "Page one. *'En bien, mon prince, so Genoa—'*"

Zzzzzzzz! Charlie Brown fell asleep right in the middle of the sentence! His head slammed down onto the book.

When he woke up, sun was streaming through the front window, and his friends were banging on the glass.

"Hey, Charlie Brown, come out and play!" Shermy called out. He was surrounded by kids holding their skates and hockey sticks.

Charlie Brown walked to the window, and his friends cheered. But he closed the curtains and went back to his chair.

"Okay, where was I?" he wondered, and he started reading again. "'. . . took a horse from a commander, and hungry and weary . . .'"

Charlie Brown read the book all day Saturday. He read it in the kitchen while he ate his lunch. He read it in the bathroom while he took a bath and brushed his teeth.

On Sunday he started reading as soon as he woke up. He settled into the living room again. When he looked up, he saw a bunch of kids sitting in chairs on his lawn, watching him read. Frustrated, he walked into his bedroom.

"Okay, show's over!" Sally told the crowd outside. "Clear out!"

Charlie Brown was still reading when the sun set on Sunday night. He was exhausted as he croaked out the last sentence.

"'. . . and to recognize a dependence we do not feel. The End.'"

He closed the book. "I did it!" he said proudly. But he wasn't quite finished. He still had to write the report!

Charlie Brown started by writing down notes on index cards. Then he tacked all the cards to his wall. He used a red string to connect the ideas. His wall started to look like a crazy spiderweb.

"If only she could see me now!" Charlie Brown exclaimed.

Finally, he was ready to start writing his report. Miss Othmar had said the report was supposed to be a thousand words.

This is my book report about War and Peace, he began. Then he counted the words. Nine!

First there was war. Then there was peace. He counted again. Now he had seventeen words.

"Only nine hundred eighty-three words to go," he said with a sigh.

But he wasn't going to give up. He kept going.

But after a few paragraphs, the metal tip of his pen snapped! The ink splattered all over everything he'd written and covered his hands.

"Rats!" Charlie Brown exclaimed. He wiped his hands on his shirt and looked for something else to write with.

"It's no use," he said, starting to get discouraged. "I'm just not as smart as they think I am."

Then he saw it, glistening in the moonlight. The pink pencil with the white feather on top, sitting in a glass jar on his shelf. He picked it up, admiring it.

"I can't let her down," he said with determination. Then he psyched himself up. "There's still time. You can do this. You can't give up on her now!"

A jolt of new energy flowed through him. He picked up the pencil and started writing again. His handwriting was neat and perfect. He looked down in awe at the paper. It was like the pencil was magic!

The pencil flew across the paper as Charlie Brown wrote. He kept writing and writing until the sun came up. Finally, he added his last three words.

"Nine hundred ninety-eight, nine hundred ninety-nine, one thousand," he counted. "Finished!"

He crawled into bed and lay down. Then he pulled the covers up and fluffed his pillow. He took a deep breath and closed his eyes.

"Wake up, big brother!" Sally yelled as she burst into his room. "Today's the assembly to celebrate your perfect score!"

Charlie Brown woke up, startled. He got out of bed and groggily walked into the living room. Sally was sitting behind a large, old-fashioned cash register. Behind her were stacks of Charlie Brown merchandise she had made herself: Charlie Brown dolls, mugs with Charlie Brown's face on them, Charlie Brown T-shirts, Charlie Brown hats . . .

"What are you up to now?" Charlie Brown asked.

"Not that you're a big celebrity, I have to move fast," Sally explained. "The fame that comes with intellectual superiority can be very fleeting. You have to cash in while you can!"

Charlie Brown smiled and gazed across the street at the Little Red-Haired Girl's house. Getting her to finally notice him—that's how *he* planned to cash in.

"Today's going to be a big day for us, big brother!" Sally said confidently.

CHAPTER SEVENTEEN
THE BIG ASSEMBLY

Charlie Brown forgot about being tired when he got to school. His report was done, and it was beautiful. And he was about to be honored for his perfect score!

Sally set up her merchandise at the entrance to the auditorium. Balloons printed with her brother's face floated above her booth. Linus and Charlie Brown walked past her to find their seats. The place was already filled with kids.

"This is all for you, Charlie Brown," said Linus, happy for his friend. "You've really made it."

Charlie Brown spotted the Little Red-Haired Girl

in her seat. She was back! Charlie Brown was thrilled.

"It's going to happen," he told Linus. "She's finally going to notice me for doing something great."

Lucy walked into the auditorium. She took in the sight of all the kids wearing Charlie Brown hats and T-shirts.

She steeled herself and walked up to Charlie Brown.

"I hate to admit it, you blockhead, but public opinion leads me to believe that after all these years, I *may* have been wrong about you," she said. "This has not been easy for me. MY WHOLE WORLD HAS TURNED UPSIDE DOWN!"

The lights went down in the auditorium, and Charlie Brown hurried backstage as everyone else took their seats. Franklin came out from behind the curtain and stood at a lectern in the center of the stage, followed by Marcie.

"Can I please have Charlie Brown come to the stage?" Franklin asked.

The spotlight found Charlie Brown as he walked out from behind the curtain to the applause of the crowd. He stood next to Franklin, who turned to him.

"It is my pleasure to present to you today, this

award, for the highest achievement in this year's standardized testing. But before I do, the school proclamation," he said.

Marcie stepped up to the microphone. "On this day whereas you have upheld the highest of academic standards, and whereas no one would have ever expected that of you, and whereas you are the first to receive a perfect score, therefore, be it resolved that today is declared Charlie Brown Day. Signed, Miss Othmar."

Franklin held out a small case. Marcie opened it and took out a gold medal. She pinned it to Charlie Brown's shirt.

Charlie Brown beamed with pride as everyone gave him a standing ovation.

"How about that, Charlie Brown?" Franklin asked. "You're the star of the school now."

The crowd burst into applause again. Charlie Brown could see the Little Red-Haired Girl out there. This was exactly the day he'd dreamed of!

Then Marcie handed him a piece of paper. "Congratulations, Charles," she said. "Let me present you with your perfect test."

Charlie Brown looked down at the test. It had his

name on it, but the bubbles had been filled in to make a smiley face! His stomach sank.

Oh no! he realized. *I must have signed the wrong paper.*

His mind flashed back to the day of the test, when he and Peppermint Patty had been in such a hurry to hand in their papers. That must have been how it happened.

Of course, nobody had to know that. He could just take his medal and go, and the Little Red-Haired Girl would be impressed. He could walk offstage a hero.

But that wasn't right, was it? He started to sweat. He tucked the paper into his back pocket and stepped up to the microphone.

He cleared his throat. "Before I begin, I'd like to thank all of you for your support," he began.

Everyone clapped and cheered.

"You have all been so kind," Charlie Brown continued. "It is not often that I get this sort of recognition."

Then he paused and cleared his throat again. "But . . . um, there's been a mistake."

The kids in the crowd started to murmur. What was Charlie Brown talking about?

Charlie Brown pulled the test from his pocket.

"This is not my test," he said bravely.

A stunned silence fell over the auditorium. Until—

"HA!" Lucy cried, jumping up. "I knew it!"

Charlie Brown finished. "Therefore, I cannot accept this honor."

Sally turned to the classmate next to her. "Can a brother and sister get a divorce?" she asked.

Charlie Brown unpinned the shiny gold medal and handed it back to Marcie, along with the test.

"I think this belongs to Peppermint Patty," he said softly.

Then he walked out of the auditorium alone.

His days as a celebrity were over. When recess came, nobody asked Charlie Brown to play with them. He sat on a bench with his head in his hands.

Linus approached and sat next to him.

"That was a very admirable thing you just did, Charlie Brown," Linus said.

That didn't make Charlie Brown feel much better. "One moment I'm the hero, the next I'm the goat."

Linus looked down at the book report in Charlie Brown's hand.

"Maybe things will go your way again after you hand in your book report," Linus said hopefully.

Charlie Brown got up and walked over to the see-saw, pacing back and forth.

"I'm not so sure!" he said, suddenly frantic. "I was up all night working on it and I can't remember a single word."

"Surely it's not as bad as you think, Charlie Brown," Linus said. "Let me see what you wrote."

Linus picked up the book report and started to read. After a minute his face lit up. He looked at Charlie Brown, astonished.

"Charlie Brown, the insight you bring to such a complex novel is beyond reproach!" he said.

He handed the report back to Charlie Brown, who set it down on one end of the seesaw. That's when he noticed the Little Red-Haired Girl enter the school-yard. She stopped and talked to a kid, who pointed in Charlie Brown's direction. Then she started walking right toward him!

"Ah!" Charlie Brown cried. He quickly put a paper bag over his head.

That didn't bother Linus. He was used to seeing

his friend with a paper bag on his head.

"You two are sure to win the gold star with a book report of this quality," he told Charlie Brown.

The Little Red-Haired Girl overheard. "Book report?" she asked. "Were we supposed to do a book report?"

"Oh, hi," said Linus. "In light of the fact that you were away, Charlie Brown took it upon himself to complete the report for both of you."

Charlie Brown shyly lifted the paper bag from his head to see the Little Red-Haired Girl giving him the biggest smile ever.

Overwhelmed, he leaned on the seesaw to steady himself. It tilted down, sending the book report flying into the air!

A gust of wind picked it up and took it higher than Charlie Brown could reach. As he chased after it, the red remote-control plane came out of nowhere! The metal propeller shredded the book report into millions of tiny pieces. They rained down on the school yard like confetti.

"Aaaaargh!" Charlie Brown cried.

He held out his hands, trying to catch the pieces of

the report. He took two pieces of the shredded paper and tried to stick them back together, but of course it was no use.

"No, no, no!" Charlie Brown wailed.

It was hopeless. He placed the pile of confetti in the Little Red-Haired Girl's hands and ran off.

"Good grief!" she said.

CHAPTER EIGHTEEN

CURSE YOU, RED BARON!

Outside the school yard, Snoopy watched the red plane destroy Charlie Brown's dreams. He shook his fist at the plane. Then he ran back to his typewriter and began to type.

Clackety-clack-clack!

```
Chapter Four: Curse You,
Red Baron!


Woodstock and his mechanics
cranked a siren--the Red Baron
had been spotted in the skies!
```

The Flying Ace jumped into his
plane and took off into the air.
He chased the Red Baron all
the way from the countryside
to the city of Paris. He never
lost sight of the red plane. He
followed it past the Eiffel Tower
and the cathedral at Notre-Dame.

The Red Baron looped around and
flew back to the Eiffel Tower.
He pulled up at the last second,
flying vertically up the side of
the tower. The Flying Ace flew
right beneath him. A drip of
oil spilled from the Red Baron's
plane, splashing the Flying Ace
in the face. He shook his head,
sending the droplets flying.

The Red Baron looped and quickly
flew back down along the Eiffel
Tower, startling the Flying Ace.
He tried to make the same sharp
turn, but his plane got stuck on
the point of the Eiffel Tower!
He stood up and stomped on his
plane, freeing it. His plane
plummeted toward the ground,
but he pulled up hard at the
last minute.

The Red Baron's plane was a red
dot in the distance now, and it
was growing dark as night fell
and a fog set in. But the Flying
Ace was not going to give up. He
bravely flew into the gloomy
fog, chasing the Red Baron.

When the fog lifted, he realized
he was behind enemy lines. He
could see the barbed wire of the
enemy camp below. Then he looked
up--and realized he was flying
right underneath the Red Baron!
His enemy could not see him. It
was the perfect cover!

The Flying Ace and the Red
Baron flew until they reached
the baron's aerodrome. Enemy
planes patrolled the skies.
Suddenly, spotlights shone on
the Flying Ace's plane, and
sirens began to wail.

The Flying Ace began to descend
to avoid the spotlights. Up ahead
he saw a wooden tower. There,
inside, was Fifi!

Their eyes met. The Flying Ace
circled the tower. Then Fifi
pointed behind him, and he
turned to look.

The Red Baron was on his tail!

The Flying Ace gasped. His plane
was hit! He was going down!

He stood on top of his plane
and saluted. She had served
him well. Smoke poured from the
engines as he landed in the
middle of the enemy aerodrome.

The Flying Ace took cover behind
the plane as spotlights shone on
him. Shading his eyes from the
brightness, he saw a zeppelin
flying overhead. Fifi sadly
waved out the window of the
airship. The Flying Ace watched
helplessly as it soared away,
accompanied by the Red Baron
and his squadron of enemy
planes, the Flying Circus.

Things were grim. It looked like
all was lost.

But he would not give up. The
Red Baron could not win! Fifi
was counting on him.

The Flying Ace stormed off into
the dark night.

CHAPTER NINETEEN

THE LONG WINTER

Snoopy walked through the backyard, passing Charlie Brown.

Charlie Brown tossed his ruined book report into the trash can next to Snoopy's doghouse. Across the street, he saw his sister selling Charlie Brown merchandise for 90 percent off. But nobody was buying. Instead, a long line of kids was trying to return their stuff.

"No refunds!" Sally yelled.

Charlie Brown retreated to his bedroom. He stared at the objects on his dresser: his kite, his baseball glove, and *10 Ways to Become a Winner!* All examples of his failure.

He shoved each one of them under his bed. And then he stopped, catching his breath. There was the pink pencil with the white feather on top. He picked it up and looked at it. Was he really ready to give up on the Little Red-Haired Girl, too?

Yes, he was. He opened his top drawer and stashed the pencil inside.

Then he sat on his bed and stared at the window. The sun set, and a bright star appeared to light up the darkness. A sliver of hope.

"Whenever I feel really alone, I just sit and stare into the night sky," Charlie Brown mused out loud. "I've always thought that one of those stars was *my* star, and at moments like this, I know that *my* star will always be there for me. Like a comfortable voice saying, 'Don't give up, kid.'"

Meanwhile, Snoopy wasn't ready to give up just yet. He started a new chapter in his book.

The Flying Ace knew he had to rescue Fifi.

Snoopy roamed the neighborhood, looking for inspiration to finish his story. He imagined that he was searching for Fifi in the French countryside.

He spotted Marcie inside her house. A friendly refuge! He borrowed her glasses to use as binoculars so he could scan the neighborhood.

He moved on. Outside another house, he heard Schroeder playing a beautiful song on his piano: Beethoven's "Moonlight Sonata." The music reminded him of the Flying Ace's love for Fifi. He howled into the sky.

He had to get closer to that beautiful music. Seconds later he popped up next to Schroeder and howled along with the music.

Schroeder stopped playing.

"No dogs allowed!"

Ejected from Schroeder's house, Snoopy walked alone through the neighborhood, still imagining he was in the French countryside. He passed Christmas carolers and snagged a scarf and hat from one of them to blend in. He couldn't risk being spotted by the enemy!

Then he spotted another house. Could Fifi be hiding there? He jumped up and grabbed on to the Christmas lights leading to the house. He moved hand over hand across the light strand so he could investigate.

Peppermint Patty spotted him outside her window. She called Charlie Brown.

"Chuck, that funny-looking kid with the big nose is over here again!" she complained.

She chased off Snoopy, who returned to his dog-house, defeated. He had no idea how to end his story. Fifi would be lost forever.

For the rest of the winter, Snoopy didn't work on his book. Charlie Brown didn't try to fly a kite. He didn't practice his pitching. And he didn't try to talk to the Little Red-Haired Girl. The boy and his dog had both given up.

Then something happened. The snow slowly melted. The days got longer and warmer and brighter. Blades of grass began to poke through the dirt.

Spring had arrived.

Charlie Brown was walking past the ice pond on a spring afternoon when . . . *wham!* A kite crashed at his feet!

He turned to see a little kid on a ladder, holding a ball of string in his hand. The kid pulled the kite back to him. Then he tossed it off the ladder, expecting it to fly. But it just crashed to the ground again.

Charlie Brown started to walk away, when the kid called out to him.

"Excuse me, mister, have you ever flown a kite?" he asked.

Yes, Charlie Brown thought. *And every time I do it, I fail!*

But the kid looked so sad, and while Charlie Brown was not the best kite flyer ever, he at least knew that tossing a kite off a ladder was not the way to do it.

"Sure," Charlie Brown said, and he approached the kid, giving him his best tips. "Wait until the wind is just right. Keep the string tight. Get a good running start. And most important of all, don't ever give up!"

Snoopy watched the whole thing. *Don't ever give up.* The words sparked something inside him.

He never should have given up on his book!

CHAPTER TWENTY
THE <u>FINAL</u> BATTLE

Snoopy rushed to his typewriter and began to write.

```
Chapter Seven: Never Give Up!

The Flying Ace knew he could
never give up on her. He could
never give up on himself.


He repaired his plane and
flew back to his aerodrome.
Then he gathered his own
squadron of Sopwith Camel
planes. They took off in the
```

darkness of night, headed for
the ocean.

Early the next morning the
Flying Ace spotted the huge
zeppelin up ahead, glinting in
the sunlight. He zoomed toward it.
The Red Baron's squadron turned
and headed toward the Flying Ace
and the Sopwith Camels.

As the Flying Ace flew closer to
the zeppelin, he could see Fifi
staring out the window of the
carriage of the airship. They
locked eyes. He surged forward
to rescue her.

Then an enemy plane appeared
behind him! The Flying Ace
ducked to avoid it, but the plane
was hot on his tail.

CRASH!

Fifi smashed a chair through
the window. It hit the enemy
plane, sending it crashing
into one of the airship's big
propellers.

The Flying Ace flew back to Fifi,
but her eyes were wide with
fear. He looked behind him to see
the Red Baron coming toward him
at superspeed.

The Red Baron fired. The Flying
Ace dodged the spray, and the
bullets hit the airship instead.
The Flying Ace didn't notice.

He flew away from the dogfight,
hoping the Red Baron would
follow him. The villain took the
bait. He followed the Flying
Ace away from the ocean, back to
land . . . where another member
of the Flying Ace's team was
waiting.

Then Woodstock leaped from the
Flying Ace's plane and landed
on a wing of the red plane. He
quickly began to unhook the
hinged panels on the wings that
helped the plane remain steady
in the air. The Red Baron's plane
lurched.

BONK!

One of the panels flew up and hit Woodstock, sending him spiraling away. But he righted himself and gave the Flying Ace a thumbs-up before he flew away. The Flying Ace nodded, then dove toward the Red Baron's damaged plane.

At the same time, Fifi noticed the damage to the airship. The envelope was swiftly deflating, and the broken propeller was sputtering and groaning. The zeppelin wouldn't stay aloft much longer. She looked for a way out and spotted an escape hatch on the ceiling. She opened it and poked out her head. The wind blew across her face.

She grabbed on to a rope and climbed on top of the carriage, slowly making her way across the top. The damaged propeller broke loose, and she stumbled. She hung on to the rope, dangling over the side of the zeppelin!

Meanwhile, the Flying Ace had the Red Baron in his sights.

He closed in on him--and then
he heard Fifi's scream. He
looked over just as the carriage
detached from the airship,
and Fifi plummeted toward the
ground.

Finish off the Red Baron
forever, or save his one true
love? There was only one choice
he could make. He sped off
after Fifi as the Red Baron
escaped.

Fifi flailed her arms and legs
as she fell through the clouds.
Then suddenly the Flying Ace's
plane was underneath her, and
she fell right into his arms.
The Flying Ace gazed into her
eyes and then looked behind
him to see the Red Baron's plane
disappear, a cloud of black
smoke trailing behind it.

The Flying Ace and Fifi came
in to land, setting down among
the squad of Sopwith Camels.
The pilots cheered for their
hero. The battle was over--for
now.

And so, as our hero observed,
he was destined to face the Red
Baron another day.

After Snoopy typed the last lines of his book, he handed the last page to Lucy. She had been reading along as Snoopy worked. Snoopy and Woodstock watched her, hoping for a good review.

Lucy read the last page and frowned.

"A dog that flies? This is the dumbest thing I've ever read!" she said, and then she tossed the manuscript into the air.

Sluuuuurp! Snoopy licked her in the face.

"*Aaaaaaagh!*" Lucy shrieked, and ran away.

CHAPTER TWENTY-ONE
THE LAST DAY OF SCHOOL

"Come on, Charlie Brown!" his friends yelled.

Charlie Brown burst out of his front door with a smile on his face. It was the last day of school!

Sally walked out behind him, wearing a graduation cap and gown.

"It's the last day of school! Well, big brother, can you believe it? My last day of school. No more reading, writing, arithmetic, ever! I can't believe school is finally over."

"What are you talking about?" Charlie Brown asked. "This is just the start of summer vacation. You have eight more years of grammar school, four more years of high school, plus four more years of college!"

Sally sighed. "Maybe I'll just join the circus."

Everyone was full of energy at school. They couldn't wait for summer to begin. And as the school day ended, one of his classmates pointed out the window.

"Look at that!" someone cried.

Over by the pond, a carnival had been set up. There were rides and games. Snoopy and Woodstock were taking a ride on the Ferris wheel.

Linus walked to the front of the class.

"Okay, everyone, listen up!" he called out. "I know this is the last day of school—"

"Yay!" everyone shouted.

"—but before we leave, we need to pick our partners for this year's summer pen pal project. When I draw a name, stand if you want to be their partner."

Charlie Brown buried his head on his desk. *Here we go again,* he thought. *Nobody will want to be partners with me.*

"All right," began Linus. "The first name is . . . Pigpen."

Patty stood up. "I will."

Violet looked over at her, annoyed.

"A little dirt never hurt anyone," Patty whispered to her friend.

Linus picked another name. "Schroeder!" he called out. Lucy grinned.

"I do!" Lucy yelled, and Schroeder cringed. "Uh, I mean, I will."

Linus called out the next name. "Charlie Brown."

The room was quiet. Nobody made eye contact with Charlie Brown. Nobody wanted him, just like he thought.

But then . . .

"I will," a quiet voice piped up.

Charlie Brown raised his head to see the Little Red-Haired Girl standing up at her desk. His mouth dropped open in shock.

"She will?" he asked.

It was real. It wasn't a daydream. The Little Red-Haired Girl had chosen him to be her pen pal! But why?

The final bell rang just as the last names were chosen. Everyone jumped up and ran out of the classroom. They raced to the carnival.

Charlie Brown followed, walking slowly behind. He leaned against a wall and watched the other kids having fun, playing games and riding rides.

Linus found him.

"Charlie Brown, where have you been?" he asked. "It's the first day of summer. You should be down there having fun with everyone else."

"I can't stop thinking about it, Linus," Charlie Brown replied. "After all the humiliating disasters she witnessed this year, why would she choose me? Was she feeling sorry for me? I don't want her to choose me just because she was feeling sorry for me. I have slightly more dignity than that."

"Well, Charlie Brown, you know my advice has always been for you to simply go up and talk to her," Linus said.

Charlie Brown nodded. "I know, Linus. I should have listened to you all along. I'm going to go right over there and talk to her."

Charlie Brown straightened up. He was going to do it, once and for all. He marched toward the Little Red-Haired Girl's house.

But as soon as he got to his street, he changed

direction and ran inside his house instead! Was he giving up after all?

No. He went to his desk and took the pink pencil with the white feather from his desk drawer. Then he marched back outside and walked up to the Little Red-Haired Girl's front walk.

He took a deep breath. "I'm turning around," he said, starting to move, but then he stopped himself. "No! Not this time!"

He bravely walked all the way to the front door. He slowly moved his hand and pressed the doorbell. The Little Red-Haired Girl's mom answered.

"*Wa wa wa?*" she asked.

"Charles, I mean, Charlie Brown," he replied.

"*Waa waa wa waaa wa waaa wa waa,*" she explained.

Charlie Brown's eyes got wide. "You say she's on her way to summer camp? I've got to catch that bus before she leaves. Thanks!"

He ran as fast as he could, rocketing through the neighborhood. Frieda, Violet, and Patty were playing jump rope, and he ran right into them.

"Hey, watch where you're going, Charlie Brown!" Violet snapped.

"Yeah, watch it!" added Patty.

Charlie Brown untangled himself from the jump rope and ran toward the pond. The crowd was so thick that he ran through the game booths to get through the carnival. He dodged softballs and plastic rings. He got blasted with a stream of water at a water gun race.

But Charlie Brown didn't care. He could see the school in the distance, where he knew the camp buses would be parked.

He dashed through a hall of mirrors, getting lost and confused for a minute. When he made it out the other side, he found himself in front of a wire fence. Beyond the fence was the street leading to the school. He could see the lines of kids boarding the buses. They were getting shorter and shorter.

But there was a hole in the fence! He could squeeze through! He dashed toward it—just as the sound of an ice-cream truck filled the air. It stopped in front of the hole in the fence, and a bunch of kids swarmed around it, blocking the hole.

Defeated, out of breath, and heartbroken, he pounded his head against a tree trunk.

"The whole world seems to be conspiring against

me," he said. Then he looked up at the sky. "I'm just asking for a little help for once in my life."

As soon as he said the words, a breeze blew up out of nowhere. The leaves in the tree rustled. A kite dropped down and hung next to him. It waved lightly in the wind.

Charlie Brown stared at it, bewildered. The Kite-Eating Tree was giving him back a kite! But why? To taunt him? What good was a kite to him now?

Then the wind kicked up again. The kite string wrapped around Charlie Brown's leg. It pulled Charlie Brown closer and closer to the fence.

Whoosh! The strongest gust yet blew up, lifting Charlie Brown over the fence and over the kids waiting for ice cream! Then he crashed back down to the ground and the kite came untied from his leg. It floated in the breeze next to Charlie Brown.

"I hope there is still time!" Charlie Brown said, and he raced toward the school. The wind blew the kite along with him.

Lucy spotted Charlie Brown and the kite from a few blocks away. It looked like he was flying the kite. Finally! He was doing it!

"Charlie Brown is flying a kite!" she yelled, and chased after him.

Peppermint Patty and Marcie were in the middle of a potato sack race, when Peppermint Patty spotted Charlie Brown.

"Wow! Chuck's got a kite in the air!" she yelled.

"Way to go, Charles!" cheered Marcie.

They hopped after Charlie Brown. More kids joined the throng. Everyone wanted to see Charlie Brown fly the kite. Snoopy saw the crowd and joined in too.

Finally, Charlie Brown reached the buses. He quickly scanned the lines of kids and saw the top of a head of red hair. He ran up to the Little Red-Haired Girl.

"Oh, hi, Charlie Brown," she said.

"You remembered my name?" he asked.

"Of course I did," she replied.

The other kids gathered around to see what was happening.

"Before I leave, there's something I really need to know," Charlie Brown said. "Why, out of all the kids in our class, would you want to be partners with me?"

The Little Red-Haired Girl smiled. "That's easy. It's because I admire the type of person you are."

Charlie Brown was confused. "An insecure, wishy-washy boy?"

She laughed. "That's not who you are at all. You showed compassion for your sister at the talent show. Honesty at the assembly. And at the dance, you were brave yet funny. And what you did for me, doing the book report while I was away, was so sweet of you."

The neighborhood kids were all moved by her words. Even Lucy started to tear up.

"So you see," continued the Little Red-Haired Girl, "when I look at you, I don't see an insecure, wishy-washy boy at all."

Charlie Brown smiled. Then the bus honked its horn.

"Sorry, I have to go now," said the Little Red-Haired Girl.

"Wait," said Charlie Brown. He took the pink pencil from his pocket. "I think this belongs to you."

She took it from him. "Oh, thank you. I've been looking everywhere for this," she said. Then she climbed onto the bus. "I'll write to you, pen pal!"

The door closed, and Charlie Brown watched the bus pull away. The Little Red-Haired Girl went to the back window of the bus and waved.

Everyone looked at Charlie Brown.

"Is he okay?" Patty whispered to Violet.

Charlie Brown smiled. He was definitely okay.

Linus walked up to him, and the other kids followed, surrounding him.

"It must feel pretty great being Charlie Brown right about now," Linus said.

"You did it!" cheered Pigpen.

"Nice job, Chuck!" said Peppermint Patty.

"Good job, Charles," added Marcie.

"Hey, big brother!" Sally said. She took a balloon from her pocket and blew it up. It had Charlie Brown's face on it. She skipped over to him. "I'm proud to be your little sister."

Lucy pushed her way through the crowd. She faced Charlie Brown with her hands on her hips.

"This time you've really gone and done it, you blockhead!" she said, in her usual crabby way. But then her frown turned into a smile. "You've shown a whole new side to yourself. Good ol' Charlie Brown."

The kids lifted Charlie Brown into the air.

"Good ol' Charlie Brown!" they cheered.